Fate had le~~ft Clay a single op~~
try. Yet he dared not let the soldiers get their hands on him.
So Clay did the only thing he could do. Reluctantly, he leaned
low over the stallion's neck and urged it on, applying the
reins and his feet. The fissure flashed toward them. He tore
his eyes off the yawning chasm and concentrated on the far
rim. Nothing but the far rim.

"Don't try it!" the officer yelled. "You'll be killed!"

White Apache paid the man no heed. Unconsciously, he
took a deep breath and held it as the stallion covered the final
few yards. The big black leaped, arcing high into the air.
Below them, the fissure dropped into the bowels of the earth.
To fall meant certain doom.

The ragged edge rushed toward them. White Apache
stayed focused on the rim. He tensed as they crashed down.
His body was jolted by the heavy impact, but he held on.
For a few harrowing seconds the stallion scrambled wildly,
its rear legs fighting for purchase on the edge. Rocks and
dirt cascaded from under its flailing hooves to plummet into
the depths below. Then, to his horror, they began to go over
the side.

9

WHITE APACHE

DESERT FURY

Jake McMasters

LEISURE BOOKS ⬛ **NEW YORK CITY**

To Judy, Joshua, and Shane.

A LEISURE BOOK®

November 1995

Published by

Dorchester Publishing Co., Inc.
276 Fifth Avenue
New York, NY 10001

Printed in the United States of America.

Prologue

The man in the shack was nervous. He paced the rickety floor like a caged cougar, one hand resting on the butt of the Remington tucked into his waistband. Quite often he licked his lips and tugged at the corners of his mustache. Regularly he prowled to the two small windows and gazed out at the somber Illinois woods in which the shack was located.

The sun had set less than 10 minutes ago. Twilight still claimed the countryside but would soon give way to darkness. A short while ago the birds in the forest had been offering their farewell chorus to the dying day. Now the woodland lay as quiet as a cemetery, the trees devoured by lengthening shadows.

Suddenly the man stiffened. Faint footsteps could be heard on the narrow path that led to the front door. Whipping out the revolver, he leveled it at the latch. When, a few seconds later, a light

5

rap sounded, he had to swallow twice before he could speak. "Who is it?"

"Who do you think?" came the haughty reply. "Let me in, Mr. Benson. It's a bit brisk out and I don't intend to catch my death of cold."

Benson was a thin man; his clothes hung on him like rags. Unconsciously, he smoothed his faded jacket as he stepped to the door and opened it a crack. "Is it really you, Mr. Randolph?" he asked, his voice cracking with emotion. "I honestly didn't think you would come."

William Randolph was not a man who suffered fools gladly. Sniffing in distaste at the foul odor that wafted from within, he gestured impatiently for the door to be opened all the way. "Of course it's really me," he snapped. "Who else would be insane enough to travel to this godforsaken spot to meet with you?" He regarded the shack as he might a pile of cow dung. "My job, sad to say, is not nearly as glamorous as most people believe it to be."

Charles Benson jerked the door wide and offered his hand. In his haste, he forgot about the Remington and nearly poked his visitor in the gut.

Randolph gave the pistol the same sort of severe look he had given the shack. "Is that absolutely necessary?"

"Sorry," Benson blurted, shoving the gun back into his belt. "I can't be too careful. There is a price on my head, you know."

"Unjustly so," Randolph said. "Or so you claim." Primly folding his slender hands at his waist, he slowly entered, being careful not to brush his immaculate suit against the jamb or the ramshackle furniture. His long nose crinkled. "Was it also necessary to pick this filthy hovel? I would have preferred a nice hotel in the center of the city."

Randolph sighed wistfully. "It has been a while since last I savored the wonderful nightlife Chicago has to offer."

"I wouldn't know about any of that," Benson said, poking his head outside. The trail was empty; the woods were as quiet as ever. Satisfied, he shut the door and moved to a pitiful excuse for a table where he took a seat. "I've been on the run so long that I can't remember the last time I was able to relax and enjoy myself."

"If you're fishing for sympathy, you won't get any from me," Randolph said. "Not until you've convinced me that you are not the callous murderer the law claims." He glanced at the two windows, then casually moved to a spot in the center of the gloomy room. "Before we go any further, I would like some light. I can't conduct a proper interview otherwise."

Benson shook his head. "That's not wise. No one knows I'm living here, and I don't intend to advertise the fact."

"My good sir," Randolph said formally, "be reasonable. There isn't another dwelling within half a mile. No one can see this place from the road, so you're perfectly safe."

"I'd still rather not."

"I must insist. If you refuse, I'm afraid I've come all the way from New York in vain. Our interview is off. Your sister will have wasted her time, and mine."

Uncertainty etched Benson's haggard features. He gnawed his lower lip for a full half a minute, then reluctantly crossed to a lantern on a peg and lit it.

"That's much better," William Randolph said happily. He stroked his neatly groomed sandy mustache and beard, then adjusted the fine, black bowler hat he wore. A long gold watch chain sparkled when he moved his coat aside to take a leather-bound tablet from a vest pocket.

"Wouldn't you like a seat?" Benson asked, gesturing at the other chair.

Randolph flipped a few pages, ignoring the question. "It was eight months ago that you beat your employer, Percy Wainright, to death with his own cane. A warrant was issued for your arrest but you fled New York City—"

"Can you blame me?" Benson interrupted. "Wainright's father has offered ten thousand dollars to the man who brings me in, dead or alive."

"What else did you expect? The man you murdered was the son of one of the richest, most powerful men in New York—"

Again Benson cut his visitor off. "Mr. Randolph, you work for the *New York Sun*. You have a reputation for being the best reporter in the city, maybe in the whole country. That's why my sister believed you when you looked her up and told her that you were willing to listen to my side of the story. She never would have set up this meeting otherwise." Benson paused. "You must know how the Wainrights made their money. They run the worst sweatshops in New York. They're vicious, evil—"

Randolph held up a hand. "Please. Everything they do is perfectly legal."

Benson could no longer contain himself. Livid, he sprang erect. "Legal?" he practically roared. "Was it legal of Percy to corner my sister in a storeroom? Was it legal for him to take vile liberties? He forced himself on her!"

"There's no proof of that," Randolph said, unruffled.

"He admitted it to me when I confronted him!"

Benson said. "He sat at his desk and laughed in my face, telling me there was nothing I could do, that it was her word against his, that if she pressed charges he would ruin her. He bragged that he would buy witnesses to prove she was a trollop!"

"So you flew into a rage and beat him to death," Randolph said. "How very unfortunate for Percy. But how fortunate for me."

Benson blinked a few times. "What do you mean?"

William Randolph took off his black bowler hat. The instant he did, a rifle barrel pushed aside the drab rags that had been tacked over the west window. Benson tried to pull the Remington, but he hardly touched it when a thunderous blast filled the cabin and the rear of his cranium exploded outward, showering the wall behind him with bits of brain, gore and blood. The fugitive was dead before his body fell to the floor.

Three brawny men bearing rifles rushed into the shack, They ringed the body. One knelt to verify that Benson was dead.

Presently, in strolled another man: a tall, elderly figure, his clothes the most expensive money could buy, his dark eyes smoldering with satanic glee. In his left hand was a smoking rifle which he gave to one of his subordinates. Going up to Randolph, he pulled out a thick wad of bills. "Here's your blood money, Bill. And I must say, you earned every penny. Everything went exactly as you said it would."

Randolph caressed the 10,000. "Thank you, Mr. Wainright. It's always a pleasure to be of service to a fine gentleman like yourself."

Wainright walked to the sprawled form, drew back a foot and kicked Benson in the groin. "That's for my son, you bastard."

Together, the reporter and the older man stepped outdoors. "Will you be returning to New York City in the morning?" Wainright asked.

"No, I'm off to Arizona after a stop in St. Louis," Randolph said.

"Arizona? Whatever for? It's a wasteland. I hear there's nothing out there but rattlesnakes and scorpions."

"There's also someone with a twenty-five thousand dollar price on his head, which I intend to collect."

"You've never failed yet." Wainright pulled up the collar of his coat to ward off the brisk breeze. "Who is this doomed soul, if I might ask?"

"They call him the White Apache."

Chapter One

Clay Taggart was a white man but he did not look like one. His raven hair had been cropped below the shoulders and tied with a headband, Apache style. His clothing consisted of a breechclout and knee-high moccasins. The sun had bronzed his skin to the point where, from a distance, he might easily be mistaken for a full-blooded warrior. Small wonder, then, that he was known far and wide as the White Apache. Or, as the Apaches themselves called him, *Lickoyee-shis-inday*.

Only his piercing, lake-blue eyes gave away Clay's true heritage. But with those eyes Clay could read in a glance more than most white men could decipher in a lifetime. Clay knew, for instance, that the three white men he was tracking had passed that way less than an hour ago, that soon he would overtake them and learn why they were so deep into the Chiricahua Mountains, where few whites ever came.

The remote range was part of a vast reservation set up by the government. It was supposed to belong to the Chiricahua for as long as the earth endured.

At least those were the terms under which the great leader Cochise had agreed to a treaty. Less than six months ago the great leader had gone to his grave believing that his people had a place where they could live for all time, a haven they could roam as they pleased. Recently, however, whites were violating the terms of the agreement without punishment. Prospectors sought gold among the high peaks. Trappers and hunters paid no heed to the boundaries. Settlers nibbled at the fringes.

At the rate things were going, Clay mused, it wouldn't be long before the treaty wasn't worth the paper it had been printed on— which was typical. Try as he might, he couldn't recollect a single treaty his former people had ever honored.

Shaking his head, Clay focused on the hoofprints in front of him. As the Good Book made plain, there was a time and a place for everything. And it would not be smart to let himself be distracted when he was so close to his quarry. If they spotted him, they'd likely set up an ambush.

The marks in the ground told Clay that two of the men rode stallions, the third a mare. From the boot tracks made when the men stopped to relieve themselves, Clay also knew that the man who rode in the lead all the time was a big, husky character. Another was skinny and bowlegged. The third wore old army boots with holes in the soles.

Clay had been out hunting when he came on their trail. That had been five hours ago, shortly after sunrise, and although his woman expected him back by noon, he was not about to give up the chase. Learning the identity of the trio was more important than having fresh meat for the evening meal. Especially since there was a very good chance the men were after him.

Clay Taggart had the distinction of being the single most wanted hombre in the whole territory. Anyone wearing a tin star, the entire Fifth Cavalry, bounty hunters, scalp hunters, every type of human predator alive—they were all after his hide.

Their reasons varied. The lawmen wanted him on a trumped-up murder charge. The army was after him for riding with a notorious band of renegade Apaches. The bounty hunters and scalp hunters were more interested in the 25,000 dollars being offered for his head than they were in seeing justice served.

None of which mattered to the White Apache. Let them come, he told himself. Let them all come. He would send them packing as he had so many already. It was kill or be killed, and he had every intention of outlasting his many enemies.

Suddenly the canyon walls echoed to the whinny of a horse. White Apache promptly ducked behind a boulder and listened for the sound to be repeated so he could pinpoint the animal's position. After a bit he heard instead the clink of a shod hoof on stone. Then, faintly, there were voices.

It surprised him. White Apache had not expected to catch up to the riders quite so soon. Wary of a trap, he cat footed forward, blending into the terrain as his Apache mentors had taught him, using the available cover so masterfully that only another Apache could have spotted him.

Clay came to a bend and slowed. The voices were louder, but he still could not make out the words. Lowering onto his belly, he snaked to the corner.

The whites had stumbled on a spring. In the shade of the right-hand canyon wall they'd made camp. Wisely, they had tethered their mounts to picket pins near the water. Two of the animals were grazing on sparse grass, but the third, a big black stallion, pranced and tossed its head.

The three men were much as Clay had imagined them to be. A hulking specimen in a wide-brimmed hat sat with his back propped against a saddle. Strapped around the man's waist was an ivory-handled Colt. Sticking out of the top of a boot was the bone hilt of a large knife.

The second man was thin enough to be a broom handle. He fiddled with a coffeepot while feeding dry brush to a greedy fire. His hat was a Stetson, and he favored Mexican spurs with huge rowels.

Last, there was a grizzled old-timer in faded buckskins. This one carried a Spencer in the crook of an arm and wore army-issue boots. A former scout, by the looks of him.

Curious to hear what they were saying, Clay wormed his way around the bend, hugging the base of the towering stone wall. Whenever one of the trio glanced in his direction, he froze. Soon he was among boulders and could make better time. As silently as a specter he closed in on his quarry, stopping twenty feet out. The tantalizing aroma of coffee reminded him how long it had been since last he had any.

"—so good," the skinny one was saying. "We've come this far without the Chiricahua being any the wiser."

"Don't let it go to your head, Bodine," said the scout. "We've been lucky, is all."

The thin man snickered in contempt. "You're

getting a mite gun-shy in your old age, Plunkett. Fess up. All these high-and-mighty Apaches just ain't as tough as you made 'em out to be, are they?"

Plunkett bristled at the suggestion of cowardice. "Go to hell, you damned Johnny-come-lately! I was fightin' these red devils since before you were born, and I say we should thank our Maker that they haven't made wolf meat of us yet." Glancing at the giant, he said, "Tell this jackass, Quid. I swear; he'll get us all killed if we're not careful."

The man named Quid was rummaging in his saddlebags. He looked up, annoyed, and growled, "If you ask me, the two of you don't behave no better than a couple of ten year olds. If I'd known that you were going to jabber like chipmunks the whole time, I never would have let you boys throw in with me."

Bodine averted his gaze, but Plunkett refused to be cowed.

"That's not fair and you darn well know it," the older man groused. "How many times have we ridden together now? Nine? Ten? And have I ever given you cause to complain before?" He did not wait for an answer. "No, I haven't. It's this kid you've brought along. He's enough to drive a body to drink."

Quid produced a piece of jerky. Taking a large bite, he smacked his lips, then said, "Simmer down, Bob. You're right. You're a good man to have around in a pinch or I wouldn't keep cutting you in for a share of the money."

"And I'm the best tracker you'll find this side of Tucson," Plunkett boasted. "All those years of eatin' lousy army grub paid off, I reckon."

Clay Taggart crept steadily nearer. He had to be extra careful because the wind was blowing from

15

him to them and he didn't want their mounts to pick up his scent. The black stallion had already been agitated by something and would not stand still. Whenever it raised its head to test the breeze, Clay flattened.

Presently Clay drew within 20 feet of the shallow oval pool. Holding his Winchester in front of him, he slowly thumbed back the hammer. The three men were so busy jawing that none heard the telltale click.

"If you're so blamed good," Bodine challenged the old scout, "why is it that you can't find hide nor hair of this White Apache we're after?"

Plunkett muttered a few curses, then rasped, "It's not as if he's going to put up a sign tellin' us where to find him. He's like a ghost, that one. They say he doesn't leave any more trace of his comings and goings than a true Apache would."

"Excuses, excuses," Bodine said.

Quid stopped chewing. "You're pushing, Jess. We can't hold it against Bob if it's taking longer than we figured. I told you this wouldn't be easy, that it might take us a long time to find the turncoat. For one third of the reward money, I think you can afford to be patient."

Bodine laughed lightly. "Hell, for that much money, I'll wait until doomsday if need be."

Clay took that as his cue. Springing erect, he trained the Winchester on them and said, "I reckon it won't be quite that long, mister."

"*You!*" Plunkett cried.

To say they were flabbergasted would be an understatement. Bodine gawked, frozen in the act of reaching for a tin cup. The scout let his mouth drop, revealing a gap where three of his front teeth had been. Only Quid recovered right away and started to make a stab for his fancy pistol before he thought better of the notion.

"Shuck the hardware, gents," Clay directed. "Real slow, unless you're partial to being lead poisoned." Tensed to cut loose at the first wrong move, he watched them shed their revolvers. Quid lowered his bent leg to hide the knife in his boot but Clay wagged the Winchester. "That Kansas neck blister of yours, too, mister."

The big man reluctantly tossed the Bowie onto the pile.

All three of them had rifles, but only the scout had kept his handy. Motioning, Clay made Plunkett throw it to one side. Then he indicated a flat spot to the left of the pool. "Plant yourselves over there while I have a look at your war bags."

Bodine glowered. "You keep your hands off our personal effects, damn you!"

"Or what?" Clay could not resist taunting. "You'll talk me to death like you do your pards?" Accenting his order with a jab of the rifle, he let them seat themselves; then he hunkered and poked through their saddlebags.

Once, the mere thought of going through another man's plunder would have filled Clay Taggart with indignation. That was before his wealthy neighbor had framed him in order to steal his ranch out from under him. That was before he had been saved from a lynching by Delgadito and the renegades. And that was before he had learned every white man in Arizona had turned against him, even men he had once called friends, men who had shared drinks with him, won some of his money at cards, or been to his ranch.

Bitter experience had taught Clay Taggart to think as an Apache would. Now he regarded all whites as mortal enemies who would gun him down on sight. That made these men fair game, as well as everything they owned.

It was more than a matter of a simple lust for vengeance. Clay Taggart had taken to the Apache way of life heart and soul. He had remade himself in their image, becoming more Apache than white, and buried the part of him that had been caused so much torment under the hard exterior of an Apache warrior.

The unwritten Chiricahua creed had become the sole standard by which Clay Taggart lived: To kill without being killed, to steal without being caught.

So it was not Clay Taggart, rancher, who rummaged through the belongings of the bounty hunters. It was *Lickoyee-shis-inday*, an Apache warrior in spirit, if not by birthright. He cast useless articles aside: extra spurs and cinches, whang leather, a deck of playing cards, and spare clothes. Boxes of ammo, though, he stacked in a pile next to the guns. When he was all done, he stuffed the cartridges into an empty saddlebag and crammed the pistols into another.

Quid studied him the whole time. Plunkett played with his beard, his brow puckered. Bodine acted as if he had ants in his britches. Finally, the young cutthroat could not stand the suspense any longer.

"What do you aim to do with us, Taggart?"

White Apache glanced at them. "I haven't rightly made up my mind yet. You deserve to be skinned alive and staked out for the buzzards to eat."

"I'd like to see you try!" Bodine blustered.

Rising, White Apache picked up the Bowie. "Suit yourself," he said, and could not repress a grin when the skinny tough recoiled and raised a hand as if to ward off a blow.

Desert Fury

Their leader unexpectedly smacked Bodine on the shoulder. "Damn, kid! Show some grit. I'm starting to think that bringing you along was a mistake. Can't you see this varmint is playing with us?"

Clay had noticed that Quid spoke with a distinct drawl of a sort he had heard before. "Texan?" he asked.

"Born and bred."

"You're a long way from home."

"Blame yourself."

"Me?"

Quid nodded. "You've become downright famous, mister. Word of the price on your head has spread clear to the Pecos, and beyond. That much money is mighty hard to resist. It's more than most folks earn in a lifetime." He shrugged. "You can't blame a man for trying."

"Yes, I can," Clay countered harshly. It had been troublesome enough when he had to contend with every local gun shark under the sun. To learn they were coming from far and wide to compete for the honor of filling him with holes made Clay realize, as nothing else could, that he would be a hunted man for as long as he lived. No matter how deeply into the mountains he retreated, or how far out into the desert he might go, there would always be greedy men willing to risk all they had for a chance at the 25,000. North of the border, south of the border, it made no difference. They would plague him to the very gates of hell, if need be.

Months ago, when Clay first started down his new path, he'd known that it would lead to more and more bloodshed as time went on. At that time he had vowed to blow out the lamps of each and every man who had unjustly lynched him, as well as take his revenge on the mastermind behind the necktie social. He had also given Delgadito his word to help the renegades in their relentless war on his former people, in return for their having saved his hide.

But Clay had never foreseen that he would become the object of the most relentless manhunt in the history of the territory. He had figured on being the hunter, not the one being hunted.

It angered Clay to think that men like Quid, Plunkett and Bodine would never permit him a moment's peace. It infuriated him that whites were sneaking onto the reservation, in defiance of the law, just for the privilege of bedding him down, permanently.

The treaty that Cochise and Jeffords had hammered out after so much effort, the precious treaty that let the Chiricahua continue living pretty much as they had since the dawn of their people, now stood in grave jeopardy because of *him*.

Just then the big bounty hunter known as Quid offered a crooked grin. "Tell you what, Taggart. How about if I give you my word that we'll leave this part of the country and never come back? Would you let us go?"

White Apache stalked up to them. The young one slid backward a few feet in blatant fear. The old one eyed him warily. Quid sat there with that brazen grin plastered on his face awaiting an answer.

"How stupid do you reckon I am?" White Apache asked Quid, then hit him. In a short, powerful stroke he slammed the stock of his rifle into the bounty hunter's face.

There was a loud crunch and a thud as Quid keeled onto his back. Both of his lips were smashed and two lower teeth were busted. Blood poured down over his chin. Dazed, he tossed his head as a great bull might, then raised a hand to his mouth. Sheer rage lit his dark eyes. Snarling, he heaved up off the ground and threw himself at Taggart.

White Apache was ready. Sidestepping the foolish rush, he drove the stock into Quid's gut, doubling the man in half, and followed through with a brutal arc to the temple that felled the bounty hunter like a poled ox.

The patter of onrushing footsteps warned White Apache of another attack. He had barely an instant in which to react. For most men, that would not have been enough; they would have gone done under Plunkett's flailing fists. But Clay Taggart's reflexes were not like those of most men. His had been honed to a razor's edge by experts in close combat. His were virtually the equal of the finest fighters on the continent, and they were certainly the equal of this occasion.

Lightning in motion, White Apace whirled and slammed the barrel across the scout's chest, knocking Plunkett head over heels. The man went down hard and made no move to stand.

Suddenly White Apache saw that Bodine was gone. He assumed the young killer was trying for the horses and shifted in that direction. Only he was wrong. White Apache whipped around at the very moment that Jess Bodine sprang at him with the Bowie he had dropped poised to strike. If not for the Winchester, White Apache would have died then and there. The big blade rang against the barrel as he jerked the rifle up. Pivoting, he dodged a wild slash that nearly opened his throat. Bodine closed in again.

White Apache simply leveled the Winchester and stroked the trigger at point-blank range.

The slug caught Bodine high in the chest and

21

catapulted him to the rear. He smacked onto his stomach in the dirt. Body convulsing, the bounty hunter tried to rise but could not. Uttering a strangled gasp, he died.

Clay Taggart surveyed his handiwork a few moments. Bending, he set to work preparing the big man and the scout. He finished mere seconds before Quid opened his eyes and sat up. The Texan started to rise, then caught himself.

"What the hell!"

Seated on a rock at the edge of the spring, Clay patted the mound of clothes, belts and boots beside him. "Are you looking for these, killer?"

Quid was livid. "You son of a bitch! What are you playing at? If you're going to shoot us, get it over with."

"I don't aim to waste another bullet on either of you," Clay revealed. Dipping his left hand into the cool water, he cupped it and took a loud sip.

Bob Plunkett stirred. Groaning, he slowly pushed up but froze halfway. "Damn!" he blurted. "I'm buck naked!" Shocked, he looked around and spotted the clothes. Insight dawned. He licked his thin lips. "The Apaches have taught you well, mister."

"Thank you," Clay said.

"You can't do this," Quid said without conviction. Squinting, he stared up at the burning sun, then at the stark canyon walls. "What chance would we have?"

"What chance were you going to give me?" Clay said. He jabbed a thumb to the west. "Tucson is that way. Start walking. With a little luck you might make it in two or three weeks."

The two bounty hunters slowly stood. Plunkett awkwardly covered himself as he shuffled off. Quid lingered to shake a fist and vowed, "Mark my words, hombre. I'll get even with you if it's the last thing I ever do."

Clay was in no mood to abide any sass. "Light a shuck before I see if your backside is bullet proof." Leaning back, he watched as they hurried to the bend, hopping and prancing like jack-rabbits whenever their feet made contact with hot stone. Once they were gone, he collected their saddlebags and rounded up their horses.

Clay did not take Quid's threat seriously. If Apaches or wild animals failed to get the pair, the merciless land would eat them alive. He seriously doubted that Quid would ever be in a position to do him any harm.

Little did he know how very wrong he was.

Chapter Two

William Randolph did not think much of St. Louis. The city was too uncivilized for his tastes, too horribly uncouth. Filled with settlers about to head west, trappers, and buffalo men and frontiersmen of every kind in from the Plains, it had a raw, primitive air he positively loathed.

The reporter preferred the finer things in life. He could not say exactly when it had happened, but Randolph had developed a taste for the very best clothes, the very best food, in short, for the best of everything money could buy.

The process had been gradual. As a top journalist in New York City, it had been part of Randolph's job to seek out and interview the rich and the powerful, the cream of New York society.

Seeing how the elite lived, mingling with them at their favorite restaurants and their clubs, letting them treat him to the most expensive liquor and meals, Randolph had found himself growing passionately fond of the tapestries of wealth. Unfortunately, he was in a profession that seldom rewarded those who made their living at it with great wealth.

So Randolph had been faced with a problem: How was he to treat himself to all the wonderful goodies money could buy when he *had* no money?

The answer had come to him quite by accident.

Randolph had been assigned to cover the story of a man wanted for several vicious robberies. The fellow also happened to have a sizable price on his head. Randolph had made the rounds of the man's family and friends, as was customary, to gather background information.

Word got back to the robber, who then sent a message to Randolph offering to turn himself in if Randolph would guarantee his safe conduct. The police, it seemed, had been upset because the man had slain one of their own, a sin New York police never forgave. They would kill the suspect on sight.

At first, Randolph had gone along with the man's request. In good faith he had arranged to meet and promised to set up the surrender so the robber would not be harmed.

Then, over a glass of wine that very evening, Randolph had second thoughts. It occurred to him that the 7,000-dollar reward would go to waste since, technically, it was for the suspect's apprehension. There had also been the murky question of ethics. In his professional capacity, he did not have the right to claim the money.

So Randolph had compromised. He had contacted the merchants' association offering the reward and discreetly let them know that he could lead their men to the robber's hiding place if they were willing to slip him the money without anyone being the wiser. They had agreed, and the poor suspect had been killed "resisting." Meanwhile Randolph had started on a new phase of his journalistic career.

In three years Randolph had made more money than in all his previous years combined. His bank account had swollen to over 100,000 dollars, and still he craved more. His goal was to have a million to his name before he reached 60. And at the rate he was going, he would achieve it.

As the carriage Randolph had rented at a livery clattered along a rough country road on the outskirts of the city he despised, he consulted the tablet he was never without. On the first page were listed the names of those who would unwittingly contribute to his growing hoard. At the top, in bold print, was the name Clay Taggart.

The carriage took a turn too fast for Randolph's taste. Poking his head out, he said, "I want to reach my destination alive, driver, if that is at all possible."

Perched on the seat was a bearded rascal in clothes fit for burning. Cackling crazily, he lashed the team with the whip so they would go faster even as he answered, "Whatever you want, fancy pants."

Randolph stewed. The man's lack of respect was galling, another example of the rustic mentality of the common herd. He was glad that there would come a time when he no longer had to deal with people like that, when he could surround himself with those who appreciated their betters.

The land beyond the window held little interest for Randolph. It was verdant farmland, too flat and green for his taste. He glimpsed farmers toiling in their fields, and he branded them as dolts for being stupid enough to accept such a grueling life.

Why did people do it? Randolph wondered. Why did they break their backs year after year to eke out a living on paltry parcels of land? Of what real value were their crude little homes? Their packs of squalling brats? Their filthy pets? In his view their lives were a total waste.

A shout from the driver drew the reporter's gaze to a cutoff ahead.

"That's the Taggart place yonder, fancy pants. You're in luck. Somebody is home."

A dirt track led to a frame house that had seen better days. From a stone chimney curled smoke. In the yard grazed a mule and a half-dozen sheep and goats. Chickens pecked and scratched. In a fenced field to the west were eight or nine cows.

Randolph hated the farm on sight.

Most of the animals scattered as the carriage rattled up. The chickens squawked and fluttered about. Only the mule was unperturbed. It went on munching contentedly.

Whistling to himself, the driver hopped down and opened the door. "Here you are, fancy pants. And you're still alive, too. Ain't it a miracle?"

"Your employer will hear about your rude behavior," Randolph said sternly, alighting. "You are a menace to yourself and others, Mr.—" he tried to remember the man's name but couldn't.

"Fletcher. Ike Fletcher," the man informed him. Arching an eyebrow, Fletcher nudged Randolph with an elbow and said, "Is it me, or could you use a quart or two of prune juice? How a person can go through life with such a sour disposition is beyond me."

Irate, the reporter pushed on past and marched the length of a narrow gravel path to the front

porch. He was about to step up when the screen
door creaked open to reveal a young woman in a
homespun dress and an apron. Instead of the ro-
bust, rough-hewn matron Randolph had expected
to meet, here was a dark-haired, delicate beauty
whose face bore more lines than her age merited
and whose lake-blue eyes mirrored an inner
strength that seemed out of place in one so frail.
She regarded him with fleeting interest, scanned
the carriage, then smiled at Fletcher.

"It's been a coon's age, Ike. How are you?"

"Just fine, ma'am," the man dutifully replied,
doffing his battered hat. "Yourself?"

"Making do." Those piercing eyes fixed on Randolph. "I'm Amelia Taggart. Who might you be,
mister? Another bill collector?"

"No, not at all," the journalist assured her, inwardly delighted to learn she was strapped for
money. Randolph introduced himself, adding,
"I've traveled a considerable distance, at great personal expense, to talk to you. I do so hope you will
extend me the courtesy of listening." Pausing, he
said conspiratorially, "It's to your benefit, my
dear. Yours, and that of your cousin, Clay."

"My cousin?" Amelia repeated in surprise.
"Land's sake, I haven't seen Clay since we were
sprouts. How is it that you know about him?"

"It's my business to know things," Randolph
said suavely. "For instance, his father, Rafe Taggart, was your father's older brother. The two of
them lived on adjoining farms back in Ohio before
Rafe headed west to take up ranching. Your father, Cyrus, did the same a few years later but settled here instead of going on to the Arizona
Territory."

Amelia had been wiping her slender hands on
the apron. Stopping, she studied him anew.

28

"Goodness, you do know an awful lot about us. Everything you say is true. My pa took up roots here because ma grew sickly. He feared going on would kill her."

"How noble of him," William Randolph said. False flattery, he had learned, gave people the impression that he genuinely cared about them even though nothing could be further from the truth. It helped him win their trust, which was crucial in convincing them to agree to his proposals. "Your father must have been a fine man."

"That he was," Amelia said, saddening. "He lost his will to live when he heard about my older brother's death at Gettysburg."

Randolph consulted his notes. "That would be Thomas, correct? He was a captain, I believe."

"Yes." Amelia's eyes moistened, and for a few harrowing moments Randolph feared she would burst into tears. To her credit, she composed herself and pushed the door wider. "Where are my manners? Come on in, why don't you? I can make some tea, if you'd like. For you and Ike, both."

Fletcher heard and started up the path, but Randolph quickly said, "No tea for me, thanks. And if you don't mind, what I have to say is for your ears, and yours alone. It's a matter of the utmost importance. Life and death, you might say." Brushing the driver off with a wave, he strolled past the woman and at her bidding walked down a narrow hall to a spartan parlor. A frayed rug covered the center of the floor. To his right stood a settee, its arms and legs nicked and scraped. To his left were a rocking chair and a straight-backed chair, both well past their prime.

The more Randolph saw, the more excited he became. Clearly the woman was in dire need of money. He seated himself on the settee as she sank into the rocking chair. Her expression told him that she was puzzled, another factor in his favor. By keeping her guessing, he could manipulate her better, all part of his master strategy.

"It must be rough on you," Randolph fired his opening salvo, "trying to make ends meet all by yourself. It's hard enough for a husband and wife to run a farm smoothly."

"Don't I know it," Amelia Taggart said. "If I had a lick of common sense, I would have sold the place for what little I could get after my pa died and gone to live in the city." Pausing, she fondly gazed at the four walls. "But I couldn't bring myself to do it. This farm holds too many memories for me just to give up. That's not the Taggart way, as my pa used to say."

Randolph nodded in sympathy. "Wouldn't it be nice if you had a nest egg socked away to tide you over during the tough times?"

Her eyes narrowed suspiciously. "Why dream of things that can't be? Wishing is for those who don't have the gumption to go out and make things happen."

Randolph found her quaint sayings rather amusing. "More words of wisdom from your father?"

"He was big on proverbs. It came from his study of the Good Book."

"Cyrus was a religious man? That I didn't know," Randolph said absently, then tensed when her mouth pinched together.

"You make it sound as if being religious is like having a disease," Amelia said. "Don't tell me that you're one of those puny thinkers who believes that the sun and the stars and all the critters in creation sprung up by accident?"

Randolph hastily repaired the breech. "Not me,

madam, I can guarantee!" he lied. "My parents raised me to have a firm faith in our Maker." Deciding it prudent to move on to another subject, he said hastily, "I was quite serious about the nest egg. There is a way you might be able to acquire, say, four hundred dollars, and help your cousin at the same time."

"Four hundred?" Amelia exclaimed, then caught herself. "What do you mean help Clay? What kind of trouble is he in that he'd need my help?"

"You haven't heard?" Randolph said. "Doesn't St. Louis have a newspaper?"

"It has several, but I can't afford to subscribe," Amelia said frankly. "Since I don't get into the city all that often, I don't keep abreast of the news."

Randolph liked to flatter himself that he planned for every contingency. Reaching inside his jacket, he removed a folded page from a recent edition of the *New York Sun*. In the center of the page was an article, written by him, detailing the escapades of the so-called White Apache. Handing it to her without comment, he waited impatiently for her to finish. Her face went pale as she read, which pleased him immensely.

Coughing to clear his throat, Randolph said, "The account you hold is my summary of all the pertinent facts as they are known. Sad to say, but your cousin is the most wanted man in the Southwest. Unless he turns himself in, I'm afraid his end will be quite violent."

"Clay did all these things?" Amelia said in disbelief. "Butchered innocent people? Burned ranches to the ground?" She vigorously shook her head. "I can't believe it!"

"Newspapers don't lie," Randolph said in his most indignant tone. Then, softening so as not to offend her, he continued, "What matters is that there might be a way to save your cousin. When I was researching his background, I learned how close the two of you were when you were little. The odds are that he still has a soft spot in his heart for you." He leaned toward her. "If you were to go to Arizona, Miss Taggart, if you were to talk to him, perhaps you could persuade Clay to change his bloodthirsty ways before it's too late."

"Go to—" Amelia blurted, and broke off. "You can't be serious, Mr. Randolph."

"Never more so."

"Out of the question. I'm sorry to say, but I just couldn't afford to."

"What if I paid your expenses and saw to it that you were given an additional four hundred dollars, in advance, for your trouble? That would enable you to hire someone to take care of the farm in your absence."

"It would, yes," Amelia said, her confusion evident. "But what is in this for you? No offense, but I doubt you're doing this out of the goodness of your heart."

Randolph warned himself to be careful. She was more perceptive than he had bargained on, but he was still one step ahead of her. "I'll be honest with you. I'm not. I'm doing this for the copy it will generate."

"How's that?"

"Journalistic parlance, Miss Taggart. Or, to put it more simply, a sensational story like this can't help but boost the *Sun's* circulation. Not to mention the boon it will be to my career since I'll be with you every step of the way, recording all that takes place for posterity."

Amelia bobbed her head. "So that's your interest. I thank you for being so honest with me."

"The truth is my byword," Randolph said, keeping a straight face.

"Then I'll be honest with you. I'm tempted, but I just don't know if it's the wise thing to do."

"I'm in no hurry," Randolph fibbed again. "Take your time. Think it over. I'll be back in the morning for your decision. If you agree, we'll leave for Tucson as soon as you arrange things here. With my knack for finding the right people, it shouldn't take us long to set up a meeting with your cousin. You can take it from there."

"I wouldn't know what to say to him after all these years."

Randolph had her hooked, and he knew it. "Say whatever is in your heart. The important thing is that you'll have tried to get him to mend his ways."

Giddy with his victory, Randolph nearly ruined it by laughing out loud. With the woman's unsuspecting help, he would lure the White Apache into a trap and afterward claim the reward. The pathetic creature in front of him did not realize it, but her cousin was as good as dead.

After the reporter left, Amelia Taggart sat in the rocking chair staring blankly at the clipping in her lap. Her emotions were in a whirl, her mind half numb. She kept telling herself that she must have imagined the whole thing. Every time she did, she would touch the clipping to confirm the truth of William Randolph's visit.

Closing her eyes, Amelia leaned back and commenced rocking gently, her toes pushing against the floorboards. Whenever she was upset, whenever her troubles proved almost too much to bear, it helped to sit in the rocking chair and sort through her thoughts.

Cousin Clay. Her mind filled with images of

their childhood together, of the many happy hours they had spent roaming the woods and frolicking in the fields. They had been as close as brother and sister, inseparable until that awful day Rafe Taggart hauled his family off to the frontier to make a new life for them.

Frankly, Amelia never had understood why. There had been nothing wrong with the old life. As she recollected, they had never wanted for food, and they always had clothes on their backs and other essentials.

Once the Conestoga carrying her cousin had disappeared in the distance, Amelia had gone off behind the woodshed and bawled her heart out. For over a year she had missed Clay terribly. Then, as time passed, the ache had eased. She had thought about him less and less.

Amelia could not even remember exactly how old she had been when news reached them that Rafe had gone on to meet his Maker. She did recall wondering whether Clay would return to Ohio. Later, she learned that he took over the ranch near Tucson and was doing quite well.

Which made the account in the newspaper all the more bewildering. Why would a prosperous rancher give up everything he owned, everything his father had worked so hard to build up over the years, and turn renegade? The only explanation she could think of was that Clay had gone insane. But that was preposterous, she told herself. Clay had always been a sober, considerate person.

Amelia read the article again, lingering over the paragraph that mentioned Clay's attempted rape of a neighbor's wife, and how he shot a man who tried to stop him. The Clay she remembered would never do such a thing. He would never stoop so low as to force himself on a woman.

Or would he?

Amelia had to admit that people could change. And it had been ages since last she'd seen him. Perhaps he had taken a turn for the worse. Maybe he had fallen in with the wrong crowd and gone completely bad. It happened, even to the best-intentioned people.

For some reason Amelia thought of Frank and Jesse James. It was common knowledge that they were the sons of a Baptist minister, and after his death were reared by a kindly physician, yet they were both notorious killers and robbers.

Absently plucking at her apron, Amelia gazed out a side window. Whether Clay had turned vicious was not all that important. No matter what he was like, he was still her cousin. They were *kin*, and the Taggart clan had always looked out for its own. In the old days, at any rate.

The reporter had a point. She might well be the only one who could persuade Clay to mend his ways. Could she turn her back on him when he needed her the most? In her mind's eye she saw Clay's youthful features, just as they had been so many years ago; she heard his carefree laughter as they raced across a meadow to see who would reach the other side first.

Amelia Taggart smiled, a wistful sort of smile for her lost childhood, for simpler days when she had not had a single worry. Life had been perfect then. In the mornings she had milked the cows and done her other chores. In the afternoons, her parents had permitted her to go off and play. Always Clay had joined her, and hand in hand they had explored every square inch of the countryside.

The memories, although long neglected, were as fresh as on the day they occurred, as crystal clear as if Clay were right there in the parlor with her. A powerful yearning came over Amelia, a yearning to see him again, to recapture some of the wonderful feelings they had once shared.

Another motive was also involved. One Amelia would not admit to herself except in her most unguarded moments. One that had caused her to spend many an hour late at night weeping softly into her pillow. One that tore at her insides every time she was outside working and happened to see a happy family go by in a wagon, or when she spied loving couples out for Sunday rides on horseback.

Amelia Taggart was bitterly lonely. Working the farm by herself, day in and day out, she rarely saw other souls except for her neighbors and an occasional friend who stopped to visit. It had taught her that of all the burdens the human soul endured, loneliness was one of the worst.

She missed having the companionship of someone who cared. She missed having someone else in the house, someone to talk to, someone to joke with. She knew that she should seek out a suitor, but she had been too busy keeping the farm afloat to make the effort.

Once, her cousin Clay had cared. Once, they had been the best of friends. As Randolph had mentioned, Clay was probably still fond of her. It was yet another reason to seek him out.

Just like that, Amelia realized she had made up her mind without being aware of doing so. She would go to Arizona. For old time's sake, because they were kin, and to ease her sense of aching loneliness, if only for a short while, Amelia would seek Clay out and save him in spite of himself.

And because she was a Taggart, Amelia would let nothing stand in her way.

Chapter Three

His name was Ken Weber and he made his living by hauling freight along the Tucson-Mesilla road. Folks claimed he was plumb loco to take a job that sent him daily through the heart of Apache territory, but Ken paid them no mind. For one thing, the army kept the Apache pretty much in line. For another, the freight company paid extra for anyone willing to make the run.

Ken Weber was no fool. He kept a Spencer handy at all times and was always on the lookout for renegades like Delgadito or the White Apache.

On this particular day, as the wagon rumbled down a knoll onto a straight stretch flanked by mesquite and cactus, Ken was about to reach for his canteen to slake his parched throat when he spotted something that moved off to the north. Instantly, he scooped up the Spencer and cradled it in his lap.

Ken was not about to stop. It was well known

that Apache were clever devils. They had all kinds of tricks to lure a victim close. Clucking, he urged the team on. The big wheels churned, raising clouds of dust in his wake.

Due to the thick mesquite, Ken was unable to see the spot clearly until he drew abreast of it. 60 yards away, in the center of a small clearing, lay a sprawled human form. A naked man. Ken placed a hand on his rifle. It was an Apache ruse, he figured, but the heathens were in for a surprise. He was too smart for them. Hiking the reins, he went to lash the horses into a gallop.

Just then, the figure weakly lifted a hand. A feeble voice bawled, "Help us! For God's sake, mister! We're white, just like you!"

Ken hesitated. The man spoke English, sure enough, but so did a few Apache. And if it was a white man, why was he in his birthday suit?

"*Please*! I'm, beggin' you!"

There was no denying the jasper was in earnest. Ken brought the wagon to a lumbering halt, looped the reins around the brake handle and jumped down. His boots crunched as he warily advanced. Mesquite soon hemmed him in, which he didn't like one bit. Every shadow hid an Apache, waiting for the right moment to pounce.

Still, Ken went on. Folks might say he was loco, but no one had ever accused him of being a coward. Sweat streamed down his face into his bushy beard as he paused to listen. Other than a low groan from the man up ahead, who had collapsed, and the buzz of a wandering insect, the chaparral was deathly still.

Finger on the trigger, Ken moved to the edge of the clearing and dropped to one knee. "Mister?" he whispered. "Can you hear me?"

The man grunted, then looked up. A thatch of

gray hair crowned a weathered face burnt nearly black by the sun. His skin was blistered, his lips puffy and cracked. He had to try twice before he could speak. "Name's Plunkett. Me and my partner tangled with the White Apache—" He was going to say more but his head sagged.

Ken Weber surveyed the mesquite. The mention of the scourge of the territory had knotted his innards. He wanted nothing to do with the White Apache. Now here was a man who genuinely *was* loco. "Is he nearby?" he whispered.

Plunkett groaned once more. Laboriously propping his elbows under his chest, he rimmed his lips with his swollen tongue and croaked, "No, no." Mustering his strength, he said, "You're safe. It was up in the Chiricahua. He stripped us and made us hike on out."

Ken's eyes widened. "You've walked all this way?"

"Me and my partner."

The reminder brought Ken to his feet. "I don't see any—" he began, but stopped on spying another sprawled figure forty yards away. "Hang on, friend. I'll check on your pard, then fetch you some water."

The second man was much bigger. Muscles corded his back and shoulders. His skin was blistered so horribly that it had peeled in many spots, allowing the sun to burn the flesh underneath.

Ken doubted this second one was still alive. Hunkering, he gingerly touched the giant's arm. Suddenly the hulking ruin flared to life. Iron fingers clamped on his wrist and he was yanked down close to a face so bloated that it barely appeared human.

"Calm down, mister!" Ken said as the stranger started to twist the arm. "I'm here to help you."

"Who—" the man mumbled, blinking rapidly in the bright light.

"I'm a freighter, on my way to Tucson. I can take you there," Ken said, thinking that would convince the man to let go. But the big man showed no such inclination.

"Where am I?" he rasped.

"About halfway between the Dragoons and the San Pedro," Ken replied. "Your pard told me that you were left afoot in the Chiricahua. Beats me how you managed it. Most would have dropped dead long ago." When the man showed no reaction, Ken commenced prying the fingers off him.

"The San Pedro River?" the man repeated thickly. "We made it, then?"

"That you did," Ken confirmed. When the giant released him, he stood. "Lie still. I'll be back right quick." Ken started to leave but halted when the man muttered a few words. Apparently they were not addressed at him.

All he heard was "Taggart" and "kill."

Clay Taggart had been astride many a horse in his time, but few measured up to the hot blood of his newest mount. The black stallion proved a joy to ride. He could go all morning at a trot, give the stallion a short rest, and gallop half the afternoon without tuckering it out. Clay had never seen the like.

Within a week of acquiring the animal, Clay had grown so fond of it that he wouldn't think of parting with it for any reason. Prudently, he told no one. Not Marista, the Pima woman who shared his wickiup, nor Colletto, her son. And certainly not the other members of Delgadito's band.

Apaches never grew attached to horses. They saw no sense in becoming fond of something they were bound to eat sooner or later. For the simple truth was that horse meat was a staple of the Apache diet.

Many a time Clay had witnessed one of his warrior friends steal a magnificent horse in a raid, only to find it roasting over a fire a week or a month later. He had yet to see a horse last more then six months in their camp.

For a former rancher, the Apache attitude toward livestock had been one of the most difficult to accept. Clay could understand how they felt about his own kind, since white-eyes had stolen most of their land right out from under them. He could appreciate why they regarded all other people as enemies to be vanquished or driven off since the history of their tribe was one long string of bloody clashes. But their callous disregard for horses, even those that had served them in good stead, was an outlook he found impossible to share.

On a sunny day, about two weeks after he tangled with the three bounty hunters, White Apache rode along a high ridge several miles to the northwest of the sheltered canyon in which the renegades were camped. He was after antelope and hoped to come upon some in one of the low valleys that bordered the Chiricahua Mountains.

It was a hot day, so hot that even the lizards and snakes had sought shade during the inferno of early afternoon. Once, not all that long ago, White Apache would have done the same. That was before he had been taken under Delgadito's wing, so to speak, and taught how to survive in the wilderness, how to find food where no other white men could, how to locate water in the middle of the driest of deserts, and how to endure the blistering Arizona sun without complaint.

Presently a winding valley watered by a narrow stream unfolded below him. Sticking to whatever cover was handy, White Apache worked his way down the boulder-strewn slope to a stand of saplings near its base. The stream was a stone's throw away, so close he could smell the dank scent of the water. That, and something else.

White Apache stiffened as the acrid odor of fresh horse urine wafted to his sensitive nostrils. Scouring the cottonwoods that lined the serpentine waterway, he noticed a wide area where the grass lining the bank had been trampled. A few hoofprints were visible.

The tracks deserved to be investigated, but White Apache was not about to ride out into the open. Sliding from the stallion, he ground hitched it, then snaked through the saplings to a belt of grama grass, where he lowered onto his hands and knees. The grass was waist high and could have concealed an entire war party. Securely shrouded, he made a beeline for the stream, poking his head into the open within 10 feet of the flattened area.

Other than the fluttering of leaves, the cottonwoods were still.

White Apache boldly stepped from concealment, the Winchester pressed to his shoulder, hammer cocked. No shots greeted him. No shouts broke out.

Judging by the number of prints, the freshness of the impressed dirt, and the fact the horses had all been shod save one, White Apache deduced that a routine cavalry patrol out of Fort Bowie had stopped to rest there less than an hour ago. Stepping to a slender cottonwood, he leaned his rifle against another, coiled, and sprang as high as he could. Grabbing the trunk, he wrapped his arms and legs around it and shimmied as high as the thin bole allowed.

No troopers were evident, but White Apache did discover a small herd of antelope grazing a mile off. Descending, he hunted for a thin branch about the length of his arm, which he then stripped of leaves and offshoots. Then he set off on foot toward them, hunched at the waist so they would not catch sight of him. The barrel of his rifle parted the high stems of grass much as the prow of a ship cleaved ocean waves.

Within several hundred yards of his quarry, White Apache knelt and burrowed under the sand and grass with the ease of a gopher. Once he had a shallow hole excavated, he drew his Bowie knife, cut a strip from the bottom of his breechcloth, and tied it to the end of the branch.

Lying flat on his back, White Apache placed the rifle beside him. It took mere moments to scoop the loose dirt over his legs and torso. Perfectly concealed except for his left arm, he elevated the branch and slowly waved it back and forth. The strip flapped lightly.

Cuchillo Negro, one of the friendlier renegades, had taught Clay this trick, routinely used by Apache to kill antelope and sometimes deer.

Curiosity, the white-eyes liked to say, was the fatal flaw of felines. The same could be said of antelope. Clay had been dumbstruck the first time he had observed the ploy in operation. It had struck him as plain ridiculous. Antelope were among the wariest of animals, able to spot movement four miles off, ready to flee at the first hint of a predator in their vicinity, human or otherwise. None would be deceived by so obvious a tactic.

Yet, to Clay's astonishment, dozens of the animals had been drawn to the waving bit of cloth Cuchillo Negro had used to tempt them in close, drawn as inexorably as fish to a bright lure or deer to a salt lick.

Now White Apache turned his head, placing an ear to the ground. He heard them long before he saw them. The dull patter of their small hooves gave them away. Presently he glimpsed furtive four-legged shapes gliding cautiously toward the branch. He did not stop waving it. To break the motion, Cuchillo Negro had instructed him, would send the animals fleeing in panicked flight, and once they were on the move, it was next to impossible to bring one down.

Antelope were the fastest animals on the North American continent, among the fleetest in the world. Vaulting in 20-foot bounds, they could race along at over 60 miles an hour for minutes at a time. No horse could keep up. And trying to fix a bead on their bobbing forms was a study in frustration.

Suddenly a pronghorn buck made bold to approach. Its wide dark eyes were fixed on the flapping strip. As if mesmerized, it walked up and tilted its head to sniff.

White Apache had to strike before the befuddled animal registered his scent. He swung the stick away from the antelope, and when it started to lean forward, he let go and looped his left arm around its neck even as he speared the Bowie into its throat. Automatically, the buck bounded backward, or tried to, but White Apache held on, stabbing again and again, slicing the pronghorn's throat to ribbons in a span of seconds. Warm blood gushed down over his chin and poured down his chest. Sharp hooves scraped at his legs. In frenzied desperation the buck half dragged him out of the hole. Still, White Apache held on. Then his forearms grew slick. He began to lose his hold. Just when he feared the animal would slip free and flee, it wheezed like a bellows, staggered, and fell on top of him.

White Apache heaved and rolled to the right. Experience had taught him that stricken antelope often thrashed madly about. In their wild convulsions they had been known to impale anyone rash enough to be within reach of their short but wicked black horns.

This particular buck sported a pair of 14 inchers, curved to the back and slightly inward. They had conical tips. About halfway up, each had a short, broad prong that jutted to the front, from which the name pronghorn was derived.

The rest of the herd was in full flight. White Apache watched them rapidly recede to the north while wiping blood from his body with clumps of grama grass. At his feet the buck kicked and flopped about until too weak to continue. Finally, it expired. White Apache slid the Bowie into the beaded sheath Marista had made for him, stooped, and hoisted the antelope onto his shoulders. It weighed in excess of 120 pounds, but he bore it effortlessly.

White Apache retrieved his rifle, faced westward, and made for the stand where he had left the stallion. The hunt had gone so well that he would be back at the wickiup before nightfall.

To the south a large red hawk soared high over the Chiricahua. White Apache felt the sun on his back and smiled. At that moment in time he felt more alive than he ever had as a rancher. His whole body pulsed with health and vigor. His muscles, once sinewy and lean, bulged with raw vitality.

Years ago, if anyone had come up to Clay and told him that one day he would be living the life of a renegade Apache and loving every minute of it, he would have branded the man plumb loco. Until Delgadito saved him from a strangulation jig, he had been much like every other white man in the territory, mistaking the Apache for vermin.

Clay chuckled. That old saw about walking a mile in the other fellow's boots, or in this case, moccasins, was as true as ever. Now that he saw the world through the eyes of a Chiricahua, he had a whole new outlook on life.

Deep in thought, White Apache reached the stream and started to wade across. A faint noise made him pivot to see behind him. For a moment he stood riveted in place, then he whirled and ran.

The soldiers had returned. Led by a saber-wielding officer, they had fanned out in a half-moon formation and advanced as quietly as possible. Their intent was transparent. Not knowing that Clay had a horse hidden nearby, they sought to take him alive by getting as close as they could and then encircling him before he could flee.

White Apache raced for the saplings, the antelope bouncing with every stride. The smart thing to do was to cast the buck aside so he could run even faster, but he stubbornly refused. He had gone to a lot of trouble to slay the animal. No matter what, he was bound and determined to hold on to it.

"After him, boys!" the officer bellowed. "Don't let him get away!"

At a gallop the troopers closed in. To a man they had their carbines out and ready for action. The young officer was slightly in the lead, his gleaming saber thrust in front of him, his features aglow with excitement.

White Apache knew that the only reason they had not opened fire on sight was because they had no idea whether he was a renegade or a tame Apache. As yet they were not near enough to note his blue eyes. To them, he appeared to be a typical warrior, and so long as he held his fire, they would probably do the same.

As if to confirm his hunch, many of the troopers commenced whooping and hollering, treating the chase as some kind of game. They thought they had him at their mercy.

White Apache was going to prove them wrong. He gained the edge of the stand, spun, hoisted the Winchester overhead, and yipped at them in defiance. Then, weaving among the thin trees, he reached the stallion.

The big black had been agitated by all the racket and had started to run off but stepped on the dangling rein and been drawn up short. It snorted as Clay slung the buck up over its back. Gripping its mane, Clay swung up, cut to the south, and jabbed his heels into its flanks.

The stallion needed little encouragement. Spooked by the yells of the cavalrymen and the thunder of scores of hooves, it burst from the saplings at a full gallop.

Harsh shouts and lusty curses greeted White Apache's reappearance. He had to ride with his body partially twisted in order to hold on to the antelope, and he saw the surprise on the troopers' faces give way to anger. They did not like being outfoxed. With their officer goading them on, they swept toward him, converging into a compact column.

"Halt!" the officer roared. "In the name of the U.S. Government, I order you to stop where you are!"

White Apache grinned. The lieutenant had to be green indeed to think that he would obey. Flapping his legs, he spurred the stallion into a draw which shortly brought him out at the base of the ridge he had descended earlier. To attempt to scale the steep slope with the army so hard on his heels would invite disaster, so he hugged the bottom and bent low, the air fanning his cheeks, his long hair whipping.

The stallion ran with a smooth, steady gait, the equal of any thoroughbred. Clay marveled again at its speed and superb endurance. He had no worry of being caught. Already the troopers were rapidly falling behind.

Then White Apache swept around a bend, and suddenly in front of him loomed a spine of earth and rock too steep for any horse to climb. He had to swing wide to the right to go around. In the process, he lost ground. A lot of ground.

The young lieutenant angled to intercept him, saying, "We have him now, boys! Onward!"

It would have been so easy for White Apache to drop five or six of them then and there. Delgadito, Fiero or one of the other renegades would have. But Clay held his fire, telling himself that he would still not shoot unless they did.

White Apache came to the end of the spine. The big black skirted a boulder the size of a log cabin. Beyond it lay an open stretch where they could regain some of the lead they had lost. They fairly flew, Clay firming his hold on the antelope which had started to slip off.

Ahead, White Apache spied a long shadow which he assumed was cast by the ridge to his left. But as he streaked nearer, he realized it could not possibly be a shadow. The ridge was to the east; the sun was to the west. There was no logical explanation for the shadow being there. Or so he mistakenly believed until he covered another 50 yards and was close enough to see the presumed shadow for what it really was. His pulse quickened and his mouth went dry.

Long ago a wide fissure had rent the earth, forming a dark abyss. The width of the cleft was uneven. It narrowed and widened haphazardly. At its narrowest, though, the distance to the opposite rim was at least 15 to 20 feet.

There was no going around it. Slanting to either side would give the troopers the chance they needed to overtake him. He might reach the end of the fissure before they did, but by then they would be so close that it might occur to the young officer to drop the stallion with a well-placed shot.

Fate had left Clay a single option. It was sheer lunacy to try. Yet he dared not let the soldiers get their hands on him. Once they realized who he was, he'd be trussed up and taken back to Fort Bowie. Whether the army turned him over to the civilian authorities was irrelevant. The end result would be the same, namely, his neck stretched at the end of a long piece of hemp.

So Clay did the only thing he could do. Reluctantly, he shoved the antelope off, leaned low over the stallion's neck and urged it on, applying the reins and his feet. The fissure flashed toward them. He tore his eyes off of the yawning chasm and concentrated on the far rim. Nothing but the far rim.

"Don't try it!" the officer yelled. "You'll be killed!"

White Apache paid the man no heed. Unconsciously, he took a deep breath and held it as the stallion covered the final few yards. The big black leaped, arcing high into the air. Below them, the fissure dropped into the bowels of the earth. To fall meant certain doom.

The ragged edge rushed toward them. White Apache stayed focused on the rim. He tensed as they crashed down. His body was jolted by the heavy impact, but he held on. For a few harrowing seconds the stallion scrambled wildly, its rear legs fighting for purchase on the edge. Rocks and dirt cascaded from under its flailing hooves to plummet into the depths below. Then, to his horror, they began to go over the side.

Chapter Four

"You want to do *what*?"

William Randolph could not quite believe his ears. They had been in Phoenix less than 10 minutes, and had only just checked into the best hotel the primitive adobe trade center had to offer. His plan was to spend one night there and no more. He was about to go to arrange for their passage to Tucson when the Taggart woman walked up to him and made her preposterous request.

"I would like to see the governor," Amelia repeated, at a loss to understand why her benefactor was so upset. He need not go along if he did not want to, but she just had to see the honorable John N. Goodwin before she talked to Clay. Her cousin's life depended on it.

Randolph hesitated. For the life of him, he could not imagine what the woman was up to. But he was dead set against her going. In order for his plan to succeed, they must keep a low profile. The fewer who knew about their arrangement, the less the likelihood of anyone putting two and two together after her cousin was killed. Recovering his composure, he inquired politely, "Might I ask why?"

Amelia almost told him. Something, a feeling deep inside, intuition perhaps, changed her mind as she opened her mouth. "I'd rather not say, Mr. Randolph. I must insist, though. You can go on about your business while I do what has to be done."

The reporter was mad enough to spit nails but he hid it well. He'd had plenty of practice on their journey west.

Of all the women William Randolph had ever met, Amelia Taggart had turned out to be the most exasperating. She was a willful woman who did as she damn well pleased whether he liked it or not.

The first time had been when he paid her the 400 dollars. He had brought cash but she insisted on being paid in gold coins. Just for her, he'd made an extra trip into St. Louis and visited a local bank.

The second time took place when they rode into the city to catch the stage. She had refused to leave until she bought a new outfit, and because she had dawdled, they had nearly been left behind.

In Denver, Randolph had arranged for a suite for the two of them. He saw no harm in sharing it since there were two bedrooms, at opposite ends. But Amelia had stubbornly refused to sleep under the same roof as him, saying it was not the ladylike thing to do. So he'd had to get her a separate room at an added expense.

There had been other incidents, minor affairs in themselves, but collectively they had aggravated him to no end. Randolph would never have tolerated her behavior if she were not so crucial to the success of his scheme.

"I'm deeply hurt that you don't trust me enough to confide in me," Randolph said, playing his part to the hilt. "But I will, of course, abide by your wishes." He bestowed his most charming smile on her. As always, it failed to elicit any response. "As for my other business, it can wait. Unless you have an objection, I would very much like to go with you."

Amelia saw no harm in it. "Very well. Let's get started."

Randolph was relieved. He had to learn what she was about and how it would effect his scheme. As they descended the plush stairs to the ornate lobby, he racked his brain for an argument he could use to convince her that it was best for everyone that they not go through with it. The best he could come up with was to remark casually, "You know, my dear, it might not be wise to draw too much attention to ourselves. There are many unscrupulous men in Arizona who would leap at the chance to claim the bounty on your cousin. If any of them should learn your identity, they might use you to get at him."

"Don't fret on that score," Amelia said, surprised that he would think she could be that stupid. "I don't aim to advertise the fact."

"Good," Randolph said. Another idea hit him and he said offhandedly, "I'll see about renting a carriage at a livery. It will take us a couple of days to reach Fort Whipple, where the governor lives." He paused masterfully. "I just hope the delay doesn't prevent us from reaching your cousin before something dreadful befalls him."

Amelia glanced at him. "Is that why you were

so upset?" she asked. "Mercy me! I wouldn't bother to go if we had to travel that far. I'm more eager than you are to see my cousin." They were passing the front desk. The clerk grinned and nodded at her, and Amelia smiled. It was the least she could do since he was the one who had inadvertently given her the idea.

"You've lost me," Randolph admitted.

"While you were checking us in, I overheard the desk clerk mention to someone else that the governor is in Phoenix at the moment," Amelia explained. "I realized that the Good Lord was blessing us with a golden opportunity."

"How so?"

"You'll see," Amelia said. She let him hail one of the carriages that always waited in front of the hotel. Once inside, Amelia made it a point to sit a discreet distance from him. Even though they had been together for almost two weeks, she could not warm to the man as she could to most folks. There was something about him that rubbed her the wrong way. She could not say exactly what. Perhaps it was his smug air, or the habit he had of being brusque with everyone except her.

"Do you know where the governor is staying?" Randolph asked the driver. Secretly, he hoped the desk clerk was wrong, or that the governor had already left.

"Sure do, mister," the man said. "Just down Central Avenue a ways. We'll be there in two shakes of a lamb's tail."

"How wonderful. Take us there." Randolph stared morosely out the window as they clattered along, blind to the bustle of activity around them as well as the scenic beauty of the nearby Phoenix Mountains. When the carriage stopped, he climbed out expecting to find a stately building worthy of housing a territorial governor. Instead, he set eyes on yet another modest adobe structure. "Are you sure this is the right place?" he asked irately.

The driver, a man who bore an uncanny resemblance to the cantankerous carriage driver in St. Louis, cocked an eye at the reporter and snorted like a buffalo. "Sure as I'm sitting here, mister. This is where John hangs his hat when he's in town."

"John?" Randolph said, appalled by such familiarity. "You call your governor by his first name?"

The driver found the question hilarious. Sobering, he said, "This is Arizona, not Washington, D.C. We're not much for being formal and standing on ceremony." He punctuated his statement with a well-aimed squirt of tobacco juice that narrowly missed Randolph's polished shoes. "Folks hereabouts don't cotton to those highfalutin top hats who think people ought to bow and scrape like slaves to their masters."

"I see," Randolph said, convinced that compared to Phoenix, St. Louis had actually been a cradle of decency and decorum. He helped Amelia down, then told the driver, "We shouldn't be long. Please wait for us."

"Sure thing. I've got nothing else to do but finish a checker game I was playing with a friend of mine."

Randolph did not care to hear it. "That's nice," he said to be civil and trailed Taggart to a small gate which opened onto a narrow walk. There were no guards, no police, no one to bar their way. It was too incredible for words.

Amelia squared her slender shoulders as she came to a door. Self-consciously, she smoothed her dress and adjusted her hat. She had never spoken to a governor before and fretted that she might be overreaching herself. The man probably had 101 important things to do, and here she was, about to bother him over a personal matter. But as her pa had always liked to say, she had it to do. Rapping lightly, she listened as footsteps resounded within.

The door swung inward. Framed in the doorway was a tall, wiry man whose kindly features somewhat eased Amelia's fears. "Yes?" he said.

Randolph stepped forward. Since he had vastly more experience in dealing with individuals of distinction, he addressed the manservant formally. "My good man, would you be so kind as to inform his excellency that William Randolph, star reporter for the *New York Sun*, and a friend, would very much like to take up a few moments of his time."

The man raked Randolph from head to toe with the kind of look a person might give one of the creatures certain astronomers claimed inhabited the planet Mars. "I *am* the governor," he said softly. "John Goodwin, at your service." He offered his hand.

Randolph was startled by the power in the man's callused grip. The driver had been right; this was no bureaucratic pencil pusher who fawned on ceremony.

Amelia swallowed as the governor took her fingers and gave them a light squeeze. Fanning the flames of her dwindling courage, she introduced herself, adding, "It's urgent that I speak to you, your honor."

Goodwin smiled. "I'm not a judge, Miss Taggart. There's no need for—" Unexpectedly, he broke off and started, as if he had been pricked by a pin.

"Pardon me. Did you say that your last name was *Taggart*?"

"Yes, sir. Clay Taggart is my cousin."

"Well, I'll be!" Gov. Goodwin declared. Catching himself, he beckoned. "Where are my manners? Come on in, both of you." He turned as an elderly Mexican woman appeared, and he spoke to her in Spanish. "I've asked Maria to bring us refreshments," he explained, then escorted them down a long, cool corridor to a spacious room containing a desk, bookshelves, several chairs and a table.

Randolph was gratified to note that the furniture was all mahogany. The man had some taste, after all. It peeved him, though, that Goodwin focused on the woman and hardly seemed to notice he was there.

"What may I do for you, Miss Taggart?"

Amelia formulated her thoughts carefully before answering. So much was riding on what she had to say that she wanted to get it just right. "It wouldn't take a genius to figure out that I'm here to see you about Clay," she began. "Only recently, when Mr. Randolph showed up on my doorstep, did I learn of all the horrible things my cousin has done. For that, I am truly sorry."

Gov. Goodwin made a tepee of his hands on top of his desk. "You have no call to apologize, ma'am. Your cousin is the one who is terrorizing the area."

"But he's blood kin, and blood, as they say, is thicker than water. I must bear some of the shame, even though I'm not the one who butchered all those poor people."

Randolph disliked being ignored, so he piped in with the query uppermost on his own mind, "As far as you know, sir, is Taggart still at large?"

"So far as I know," Gov. Goodwin said. "But you

must understand that it can take a long time for word to trickle to Phoenix or Fort Whipple from down Tucson way, and even longer from Fort Bowie."

Amelia was encouraged by the news. Her main fear during the trip west had been that Clay would be killed before she was able to track him down. "Mr. Randolph tells me that a large reward is being offered."

"Yes, ma'am. Twenty-five thousand dollars." Goodwin hesitated, then finished with, "Dead or alive."

"Is there anyone you know of who wants to bring Clay in alive?"

The governor leaned back, his brow puckered. "Since you're not one to mince words, Miss Taggart, neither will I. No, I doubt very much if there is a single soul in Arizona who would go to that much effort. I don't mean to upset you, but your cousin is the most hated man alive. Most of our citizens would as soon slit his throat as look at him."

"I expected as much," Amelia said. "Yet the very reason I am here is to try to talk Clay into turning himself in without more bloodshed."

"I wish you luck. Frankly, I think you're wasting your time. When did you last see your cousin?"

"We were about ten."

Gov. Goodwin let out a sigh. "Miss Taggart, please bear in mind that what I say next is meant to spare your feelings. You have come a long way with the very best of intentions, but I feel you are setting yourself up for a disappointment that will tear you in two." Bending, he opened a drawer and removed a stack of papers several inches thick. "Do you see these? Each and every one is a report of an atrocity committed by your cousin, both on our side of the border and down in Mexico. He has raided ranches, slaying whole families and burning the buildings to the ground. He has attacked wagon trains, random travelers, prospectors and cowboys, even cavalry patrols."

Amelia was staggered by the number. "I knew there were a lot, but that many?"

The governor tapped on the stack. "Granted, not half of these are confirmed accounts. Most are hearsay. Some, undoubtedly, were committed by other renegades and chalked up to your cousin. But the point I am trying to make is that the man you seek is not the little boy you once knew. He is a cold-hearted fiend who might well add you to his growing list of victims."

"I can't believe Clay would ever harm me."

"Are you being realistic?" Goodwin challenged her.

Amelia refused to be cowed. "I reckon I won't know until I meet him face-to-face." Straightening, she opted to get right to the point of her visit. "And that's where you come in, sir. I was hoping you could help me out in that regard."

Gov. Goodwin glanced at Randolph, who shrugged to show he was as much in the dark as the head of the territory. "Can you be more specific, ma'am?"

"I came here to ask if you would see fit to grant my cousin your protection if he turns himself in."

Goodwin was stupefied.

So was William Randolph. Never in a million years would he have suspected her true motive. It was so ludicrous, he reflected, that only a hick like her would have thought of it. Had he known, he would have kept her from coming at any cost.

"Hear me out," Amelia said, afraid that the governor would make her leave for having the audacity to impose upon him. "As you yourself just pointed out, the moment Clay shows his face he's liable to be gunned down. But not if I had a paper from you guaranteeing he would not be harmed."

"You can't be serious," Gov. Goodwin said.

"Never more so."

Randolph squirmed in his chair. A safe-conduct pass from the governor would spoil everything. It was the legal equivalent of temporary amnesty, and anyone who shot the White Apache might not be eligible to collect the reward.

Amelia could tell that the governor was against the idea, so she quickly pressed her point. "What have you got to lose, sir? The important thing is to put an end to the bloodshed, isn't it? Well, Clay will never turn himself in knowing that he'll be killed doing so. But he just might if I can persuade him that no one will lift a finger against him."

"Your cousin is no fool. Do you honestly think he'll go to all the trouble of surrendering, only to be hung?"

"No, but he'll do it if you give me your word that instead of hanging, he'll spend the rest of his life in prison."

"Miss Taggart, you ask too much."

"Do I?" Amelia persisted. "Even if it means saving countless lives?"

Their eyes met, and locked.

At the northern edge of the Chiricahua, a cleft in the earth nearly brought about what the good people of Arizona wanted more than anything else: the death of the White Apache. As the black stallion's flying hooves lost their purchase on the south rim, Clay Taggart and his mount started to go over the edge. Another few inches was all it would have taken. But at the very last moment, at the brink of their destruction, the stallion frantically righted itself and bounded into the clear.

Clay laughed. The close call had set his pulse pounding. Intoxicated by the heady excitement, he galloped toward the foothills, swiveling to check on his pursuers.

The troopers had halted at the fissure. Few could hide their amazement at his deliverance. The young officer peered into the murky abyss, then looked at Clay. Rising in his stirrups, he snapped his saber in a sincere salute.

It was a grand gesture, an acknowledgement of Clay's courage and riding skill. Clay waved his Winchester in return but decided that was not enough. Slowing, he cupped a hand to his mouth and shouted, "Better luck next time, blue bellies! Give my regards to Col. Reynolds!"

They knew then. He had given his identity away as surely as if he had hollered his name. They became excited, gesturing and jabbering, some wheeling to the right and the left to go around the fissure. The officer wisely stopped them since it was plain they had no hope of catching him.

Clay knew he had made a mistake in revealing who he was. The army had made his capture or elimination a top priority. Once the officer in charge at Fort Bowie, Col. Reynolds, heard the lieutenant's report, a half dozen more patrols would be sent into the area to hunt him down. Delgadito's band would be forced to lie low.

Clay wasn't very worried. He doubted the troopers would locate the renegade sanctuary, hidden in a remote valley known only to a handful of Chiricahua, whose dislike of all whites prevented them from revealing the secret.

Clay's only regret was the loss of the antelope. Three days later, when he reached the hidden entrance to the valley, a pair of plump rabbits and a small doe were draped over the back of his horse.

A ribbon of a trail wound among massive boulders that were so high, they blotted out the sun. Clay threaded the stallion through, at times having to lift one leg or the other to avoid scraping them. Soon the trail broadened. He entered the verdant valley and reined up to scan the heights above.

There had been a time when Clay would not have spied the lookout, so expertly did the warrior blend into the background. Now, his keen eyes detected the outline of a human head screened by brown weeds. Clay hoisted his rifle in greeting.

Ponce, the youngest renegade, showed himself. In the Chiricahua tongue he called down, "It is good you have come back, *Lickoyee-shis-inday*. There has been trouble. Fiero and Delgadito have argued, and Fiero says he is leaving in the morning."

"Thank you for the warning," Clay responded in kind. Although he had the habit of accenting the wrong syllables on certain words, diligent effort on his part had resulted in a fluency in the Chiricahua language few whites could equal.

Clucking to the stallion, White Apache trotted toward cottonwoods that rimmed the spring which fed the valley. Presently he saw five wickiups. Figures moved about. Most were women. Mexican women.

It had been White Apache's idea to venture into Sonora and attack a large *conducta* for the purpose of obtaining wives for the four warriors.

His purpose had been twofold, companionship being the most obvious. Without women, the warriors had been growing more and more restless, and restless men were careless men.

Since Delgadito and the others were considered outcasts by the Chiricahua, and no Chiricahua women would have anything to do with them, stealing Mexican women had seemed the natural thing to do.

The Apache had been doing so for generations. They much preferred Mexican women to white women for the simple reason that white women seldom lasted long in captivity. Most would rather die than let a warrior take advantage of them. The few who submitted never wholeheartedly gave in and were always seeking an opportunity to escape. They were, in short, more trouble than they were worth.

Mexican women were different. It wasn't that they were more docile than their sisters to the north. Nor were they weaker in any respect. No, White Apache had come to understand that Mexican women made excellent Apache wives because of the raw terror the Apache inspired in them; they were too afraid to resist.

To understand, one had only to realize that decades of Apache raids into Mexico had instilled a fear so deep and widespread in the Mexican people, that the mere mention of an Apache band being on the prowl was enough to make them bolt their doors and windows until the peril had passed.

Where white women regarded Apache as plain vile savages, Mexican women had been raised to view Apache as savage demons, as virtual ghosts who flitted about the countryside with impunity, as supernatural fiends who delighted in carving the warm, beating hearts from living victims. Utter dread made Mexican women ideal captives.

The second reason White Apache had insisted on the raid had to do with Delgadito's desire to see the band grow. Few whites were aware that renegade bands invariably included women and children. No band without them ever lasted long. By taking the Mexican women as wives, Delgadito's band demonstrated to their reservation brothers that the band was prospering, that it was safe for others to bring their families and join the renegade cause.

So far, though, no one had done so. Clay reckoned that it would take a while yet before the band's numbers swelled. The way he saw it, a few more bold, successful raids would do the trick. Once word spread, warriors would come from far and wide to help drive the whites from their homeland. In the bargain, they would help him take his revenge on the vermin who had tried to string him up.

But now Clay's scheme was in jeopardy. If Fiero left, there would only be three of them. It might influence others not to join. Maybe the band would even fall apart. And if that happened, his carefully laid scheme to get revenge on the man who had stolen his ranch and the woman he loved would be ruined.

He could not let that happen.

Chapter Five

The five wickiups, made from brush and grass, layered over a framework of slender poles, were arranged in a circle in a clearing beside the spring. Seated outside one of them was Delgadito's woman, Alexandra, a big-chested woman who had crafted herself a baggy dress from deer hide. She was busy weaving a basket that would be used to store food.

Kneeling by the stream was the woman Cuchillo Negro had claimed. Florencio was her name, and of all the captives, she had adapted best to their new life. Already she had learned many Apache words and phrases, and before long she would be fluent enough to hold regular conversations.

Standing outside White Apache's dwelling were Marista, the Pima outcast who had become his mate, and Fiero's woman, Delores Garcia. Garcia had streaks of gray in her hair and was as thin as a rail, but she also had an inner toughness that made her a match for the hotheaded warrior who had stolen her.

Nearby, mending a broken bowstring was Coletto, Marista's son.

Marista glanced around as White Apache entered the clearing, her long raven hair glinting luxuriously in the sunlight. Her smile of welcome warmed his heart. In imperfect English she had learned from Dr. David Wooster of San Francisco, a physician who had once lived among her people, she said, "My heart be glad to see you safe, *Lickoyee-shis-inday*."

Clay tossed the rabbits at her feet. "And I am happy to be back," he answered. Sliding down, he nodded at Coletto, who only smiled. The Pima boy had been trying his utmost to emulate the Chiricahua, and since it was unseemly for an Apache warrior to display strong affection in public, neither did he.

Delores Garcia spoke little Apache and less English. She did say, "Hello, White Apache."

"*Buenos tardes, senorita,*" Clay said. His Spanish was limited, but he knew enough to say, "I hear your man wants to leave us."

"*Si,*" Delores said, her disappointment as evident as her large hooked nose.

"*Por que?*"

"He says he is tired of hiding in these mountains. He says he wants to go kill white-eyes and *Nakai-yes*. He says Delgadito and you and the other men are content to live like women, but he is not. So we leave at first light."

"He is taking you with him?"

Delores gazed wistfully at the wickiups. An unattractive middle-aged widow, she had been wasting her life away in Mexico, where no man wanted her, at the time she had been abducted. She had been so grateful to Fiero for saving her from her lonely life of drudgery, that she actually liked being the firebrand's woman. "Where he goes, I go."

"Where is he?"

Marista nodded toward a knoll to the north. "They try make Fiero stay."

Without another word, White Apache hurried off. He heard no voices and figured that he had arrived too late to join in, but on reaching the top, he found the three warriors seated there, Fiero glowering at Delgadito and Cuchillo Negro while the latter two stared at the temperamental warrior in frank annoyance.

Delgadito was an exceptionally tall, superbly muscled warrior. His black hair was bound at the forehead by a strip of cloth. He had a wide, smooth brow, riveting eyes, and a thin, tight—some might have said cruel—mouth. A long-sleeved shirt covered his chest. He also wore a breechcloth and high moccasins typical of his people.

Cuchillo Negro was shorter and stockier, but his style of dress was identical. His name meant black knife. He had earned it years ago after slaying a formidable *nakai-yes*, or Mexican, in a hand-to-hand knife fight. Afterward, Cuchillo Negro had claimed the man's black-handled blade as his own. As a result of that clash and many others, he was generally believed to be the best knife fighter in the entire Chiricahua tribe.

Fiero lived up to his name. He was almost as tall as Delgadito but much more broad through the chest. And where Delgadito was sinewy, Fiero, rare for an Apache, bulged with rippling muscles. His dark eyes were set uncommonly close together. On his forehead, he bore a scar in the shape of a lightning bolt, the legacy of a fight with scalp hunters.

"*Lickoyee-shis-inday*, he said in greeting. "You have come in time to hear my decision."

White Apache sank cross-legged to the ground and rested his .44-40 across his legs. "I have already heard. You are leaving. I will be sorry to see you go."

Fiero was puzzled. He had counted on White Apache being upset, on his white-eye brother making a plea for him to stay. "You do not care?"

"My people have a saying," White Apache said, and translated it as best the Chiricahua tongue allowed. "A true man does what he has to do. If you are tired of fighting to free your people, that is your choice. I hope you will be happy living as a reservation Apache."

The insult was almost more than Fiero could bear. Flushing scarlet, he said, "I will never live as a reservation cur! I would rather die first!"

Countless disagreements had taught White Apache to pick his words carefully when dealing with the firebrand. Pretending to take no notice of Fiero's agitation, he said, "I see. You plan to go live down in Mexico. That is very smart. You will be safer there. Perhaps we will come and visit you when time allows."

For anyone to imply that Fiero valued his personal safety over all else was a slight on his manhood. When charging enemies, he was always foremost. In battle, he was always in the thick of the fight. Every Chiricahua, male or female, knew there was none braver than Fiero. "You saved my life once," he said, "or I would shoot you."

"What have I done?" White Apache asked, feigning innocence.

"I go to hunt the white-eyes, to slay them as they

have slain my people, to show them that so long as a single Chiricahua refuses to give up, they have not won."

White Apache was in no rush to respond. The more Fiero stewed and the more flustered he became, the easier it would be to bend the warrior to his will. "How strange. We all want the same thing, and in numbers there is strength. You know this, yet you want to desert us."

Cuchillo Negro had to look away so Fiero would not see the laughter in his eyes. The cleverest of the band, he could see what their white friend was up to. It was yet another example of why he believed White Apache made a better leader than Delgadito.

The warrior in question also saw through Clay Taggart's tactic, but he was nowhere near as pleased. Of late, the members of the band relied more on Clay Taggart's judgment than his own, which disturbed him greatly. He was the one who had organized the band. He was the one who had been its leader until Sonoran scalp hunters nearly wiped them out. Now, for all intents and purposes, White Apache was in charge. It should not be.

"I desert no one," Fiero was saying. "I go to do that which we agreed to do: fight white-eyes. It is the rest of you who have forgotten why we joined together. It is the rest of you who are content to sit around like women, telling stories and sharpening your knives when you should be sticking them in the bellies of our enemies."

White Apache brandished his Bowie, tilting the blade so it mirrored the bright sun. "I, too, want to bury my blade in my enemies. That is why I head south tomorrow on a raid." He glanced at Black Knife. "Will you join me, Cuchillo Negro?"

"Yes, *Lickoyee-shis-inday*."

"And you, Delgadito?"

The former leader struggled to hide his resentment. "Yes," he said.

"And Ponce will come, too," White Apache said. He faced the firebrand and sighed. "Which means you are the only one who will not be going. We will miss you. But we know you do what is best for you."

Fiero's mouth creased in a rare smile. He did not really want to leave. By claiming he would, his purpose had been to force the others into agreeing to another raid. And here *Lickoyee-shis-inday* had played right into his hands! Filled with glee at how clever he had been, he said, "When my brothers need me, am I not always there? If you go on a raid, I will be at your side."

"You will stay with the band, then?" White Apache asked.

"I will stay." Fiero rose. "I go to tell my woman before she packs all we have."

As the hothead departed, Delgadito plucked a stem of grass and placed it between his lips. "You have done well, *Lickoyee-shis-inday*," he complimented his adversary. "Let us hope that Fiero never learns how you have tricked him all these times." Rising, he likewise departed.

Clay did not open his mouth again until he saw Delgadito reach the wickiups. "Do you think that was a threat?" he asked his friend.

"What do you think?" Cuchillo Negro rejoined. "I have warned you before not to trust him. His knife, like Fiero's and yours, thirsts for blood." The warrior paused. "Your blood, *Lickoyee-shis-inday*."

* * *

At that very moment, Benjamin Quid stood at the bar of his favorite water hole in Tucson and glumly lifted a glass. The coffin varnish burned a patch down his throat to his stomach, but he did not enjoy it as much as he normally would.

Quid had not enjoyed much of anything since tangling with the White Apache. During the grueling trek through the parched wilderness, all he could think of was one day soon savoring sweet revenge.

The humiliation burned within him, festering, growing more and more as the days went by. Now his every waking moment was soured by the realization that Clay Taggart had gotten the better of him. No one had ever done that before. It rankled, as nothing else ever had. It made him constantly bitter, toward himself and the world in general.

If it was the last thing he ever did, Quid resolved while downing more whiskey, he would pay the renegade son of a bitch back. He didn't know how. He didn't know when. But he wouldn't rest until he had.

As Quid lifted the bottle to pour more red-eye, he happened to glance out the window and spy the steeple atop one of Tucson's churches, several blocks distant. Without giving any thought to what he was doing, he said under his breath, "I'd be willing to give my soul to the devil for a chance to get back at that bastard!"

Hardly were the words out of the bounty hunter's mouth than a grizzled figure in buckskins stepped through the door and hastened over to him.

Bob Plunkett had fared better than Quid during their ordeal. A lot of it had to do with the old scout being as hard as rawhide and as mean as a riled grizzly.

Plunkett's mean streak was the reason he had lost his job as an army scout back in Texas. A captain had caught him with a young Kiowa girl, taken one look at her bound, bleeding form, and hauled Plunkett up before the commanding officer at Fort Richardson.

Quid knew that the old man had saved their lives. Had Plunkett not spotted the freighter, they would have died out in the mesquite. It was yet another thorn in his side, because it made him beholden to the scout. And Quid hated owing any man. "What do you want?" he demanded gruffly.

"I have some news you might like to hear," Plunkett said. He had ridden with the big bounty hunter long enough to know how moody Quid could be when under the influence of bug juice. But since he had made more money in the few years they had been partnered up than in all the years he had worked for the army, Plunkett took the foul moods in stride.

"Go away," Quid said. "I still have half of this bottle to finish, and I don't want to be disturbed until I'm done."

Plunkett did not budge. "Not even if it concerns the White Apache?"

Quid squinted at the old coot. "Don't tell me someone else has claimed the bounty?"

The scout leaned on the bar, then glanced both ways to ensure no one else was close enough to overhear. He didn't want to risk his secret becoming common knowledge. They weren't the only ones after Clay Taggart. "No, nothing like that," he said quietly.

"Then what?" Quid snapped, wishing Plunkett would go away and leave him alone so he could drink himself into a stupor as he had done every day since they arrived in Tucson. It helped ease the gnawing rage that was eating him alive.

Plunkett leaned closer, smirking in anticipation of his pard's reaction.

"Well?" Quid goaded. "Get on with it."

"You'll never guess who just checked into the very hotel we're stayin' at," the scout said to draw out the suspense. He was enjoying himself immensely.

Quid came close to losing his patience. "Who?" he asked testily, not really caring. Tired of Plunkett's silliness, he raised the glass one more time.

"Clay Taggart's cousin."

The bounty hunter went as rigid as a board. Then, aglow with an inner fire, he whirled and smacked the glass on the counter so hard that half the whiskey spilled. "The hell you say!" he exclaimed.

Plunkett scanned the other patrons, a few of whom had looked up at Quid's outburst. "Keep your voice down," he said, "unless you want the whole blamed town to find out."

"Are you sure about this?" Quid asked. "So far as anyone knows, he doesn't have any kin."

Dropping his voice to a whisper, the scout said, "I was in the lobby, watchin' for this girl who goes by every day about this time, when in walked a dude and a pretty filly." Plunkett snickered. "You should see the dude! The yack is wearin' a suit so stiff, the clothes could stand up without him in 'em. He struts around like one of them peacocks, talkin' down his nose at anyone and everyone. I'd sure like to—"

Quid did not give a royal damn about the dandy. Grabbing the scout's arm, he growled, "The filly, Bob. I want to hear about the filly."

Plunkett shrugged free. To have others touch him was distasteful, even his few friends. "All right, simmer down." Again he checked the nearest patrons. None showed any interest. "So there I was, starin' out the window, when I heard the woman tell the desk clerk that her name was Amelia Taggart. The clerk looked as if he were going to choke. He asked if she were any relation to Clay Taggart, and she up and admitted that she's his cousin, come all the way from St. Louis to see him."

"I'll be damned," Quid said, astounded by their stroke of luck.

"I felt the same way," Plunkett said. "I was hopin' to learn more, but the dude whisked her up the stairs before the clerk could ask more questions. I got the idea that the dude wasn't too happy about her spoutin' off like she'd done."

Quid immediately thought of the other bounty hunters after Taggart's hide. "The clerk will probably spread it around, and by nightfall the whole town will know."

"Maybe not. No sooner did the dude take the filly to her room than he was back again. I heard him ask the clerk not to let the cat out of the bag. A few bills exchanged hands. The dude hinted there would be more if they could get out of Tucson without anyone being the wiser."

"Smart man, this dude."

"I wonder what they're up to?" Plunkett said.

"Let's find out."

Quid paid the barkeep and strolled out into the blazing sun. Pulling his new hat low, he turned to the left and almost bumped into a sturdily built man ambling along the boardwalk.

It was the town marshal.

Marshal Tom Crane had a reputation for being

tough. Rumor had it that when bucked, he could turn downright vicious—which had made Quid all the more suspicious when, after hearing of their recent plight, the lawdog had come by the sawbone's office to ask how they were faring and to wish them well.

Now Crane hooked the thumb of his right hand in his gun belt next to the well-worn butt of his Colt, idly stroked his waxed mustache with his left, and said, "Howdy, gents. I see you're both feeling a lot better."

"That we are," Plunkett said.

Quid merely nodded. He had a hunch that there was more to the lawman's seeming friendliness than Crane let on, although what it might be, he couldn't say. On the sly he had asked around, but the only interesting fact he had gleaned was that Crane was in the pocket of a wealthy local rancher named Miles Gillett, the same Gillett who had kindly offered to foot the bill for the clothes Plunkett and he were wearing.

What made it more interesting was that Miles Gillett happened to be the husband of the woman Clay Taggart supposedly tried to rape before being forced to flee into the mountains, where he somehow hooked up with renegade Apache. And it had been one of Gillett's men who Taggart gunned down while escaping.

Quid liked to flatter himself that he knew human nature inside and out. Having lived most of his life on the thin edge that separated the law abiding from the lawless, he could smell something crooked a mile away. And his inner nose told him that the business with Gillett's wife and Taggart reeked to high heaven.

"I see you got yourselves new outfits," the marshal was saying. "What did you do? Rob the bank?" A hint of a grin curled his neatly trimmed mustache, but there was no humor in it, no warmth. It was the grin of a wolf before it attacked.

"Not hardly," Plunkett said. "An hombre named Gillett sent word that we were free to help ourselves to whatever we needed from Anderson's General Store and Feed. I reckon he heard about our fix and took pity on us."

"Mr. Gillett did that?" Marshal Crane said, and suddenly he was as friendly as could be, clapping the scout on the back as if they were the best of acquaintances. "Well, that's Miles for you. There isn't a more decent man in the territory. The salt of the earth, he is."

Quid decided to pry without being obvious. "I sent him a note saying how grateful we were, but Gillett never answered it."

"He's a busy man," Crane said. "Or didn't you know that he owns the largest ranch in these parts?"

"So I heard tell," Quid said. Acting casual, he added, "Weren't Gillett and Clay Taggart neighbors at one time?"

The lawman nodded. "That they were, until the turncoat bastard tried to rape Gillett's wife." His features clouded. "Who would have thought that Taggart would hook up with Delgadito's bunch? For the life of me, I can't figure out how it came about. Delgadito hates whites."

Quid already knew all there was worth knowing about the renegades. He was more interested in something else. "What happened to Taggart's ranch after he turned bad?"

Crane stroked his mustache again. "Miles bought it for pennies on the dollar." He snickered. "I'd say that served Taggart right after all the grief he caused Mr. Gillett, wouldn't you?"

"There is justice in the world, after all," Quid said, masking his true feelings. Suddenly he saw the whole affair in an entirely new light. Any man who could keep a vicious lawdog like Tom Crane on a tight leash had to be even more vicious himself. Which meant that Miles Gillett was not quite the saint Crane made the man out to be.

If Quid was right, it explained a lot. Gillett might have set Taggart up to get his greedy hands on Taggart's land. No wonder Clay Taggart had crossed the line. To confirm his hunch, he said, "Is there any truth to the reports I've heard that the White Apache likes to raid ranches around Tucson? It might help me track him down, if so."

Marshal Crane spat in the dust. "It's true, unfortunately. A rancher named Prost and another, Jacoby, were dragged from their beds in the middle of the night and murdered."

Quid was going to ask if they were friends of Gillett's, but the lawman abruptly touched his hat brim and tromped off.

"I've got work to do, gents. Be seeing you around."

Bob Plunkett was glad to see the lawman go. Eager to get to the hotel and learn why Taggart's cousin was in Tucson, he turned to hurry off. To his utter surprise, the very man they needed to talk to was walking toward them. "It's him!"

"Who?" Quid asked, still watching Crane.

"Who else? The dude."

William Randolph had his hands clasped behind his back and his head bowed. He was beginning to think that trying to claim the bounty on the White Apache was the biggest mistake he had ever made. Nothing had gone right. Amelia had persuaded Gov. Goodwin to issue a safe-conduct pass. Once it was in Taggart's hands, killing him would be out of the question.

The reporter refused to concede defeat. He had too much time and money invested in the venture to back down. Somehow, he mused, there had to be a way to thwart the governor's intervention.

The solution hit him like a ton of bricks. Stopping short, Randolph smiled. It was so simple! All he had to do was arrange for Taggart to be slain *before* Amelia made contact. The reward would still be in effect. He would get his hands on the $25,000, after all.

But how to go about it? Randolph wondered. Where was he going to find someone deadly enough to do the job on such short notice? He had hoped to stall the woman long enough for him discreetly to seek a likely prospect, but she was determined to leave in the morning.

Just then a shadow fell across him. Randolph stopped and looked up into the flinty face of a broad-shouldered man in a wide-brimmed black hat. The stranger wore an ivory-handled Colt on one hip and a large knife in a leather sheath on the other.

"We need to palaver, mister," the hardcase declared. "And I won't take no for an answer."

William Randolph smiled. Something told him that his prayers had just been answered.

Chapter Six

The renegades had been traveling south for six straight days when they came upon tracks made by three heavily laden wagons and a half-dozen riders winding along the border of the Chiricahua reservation. The tracks led farther south, toward Mexico.

Since the wagons avoided the only road in the area, and since the party always made camp in out of the way places where they were unlikely to be noticed by roving cavalry patrols, Clay deduced that the wagons belonged to one of the many bands of smugglers operating in the region.

It was no secret that a thriving illegal trade flourished between criminal elements in southern Arizona and northern Mexico. Rifles, pistols and ammunition were routinely smuggled across the border, as were cattle, horses and other livestock.

Years ago, before the coming of the whites, the Spanish had seen fit to enslave members of various Indian tribes. Men, women, even children had been marched south in chains and made to work in mines or labor on vast haciendas. They were treated like animals, given barely enough food to survive and worked to the point of exhaustion day in and day out. Not surprisingly, few of the Indians lasted very long.

The American Government had tried to put a stop to the slave trade. But the cavalry could not be everywhere at once. The border was so long, the region so remote, that those who operated outside the law continued to do so with virtual impunity.

Clay Taggart was glad they had stumbled on smugglers and not unsuspecting families on the move. Although raiding was part and parcel of the Apache way of life, and killing without being killed was one of the highest Apache virtues, he balked at the notion of wiping out innocent pilgrims.

The band stuck to the trail like a pack of wolves on the scent of a deer herd. As was the Chiricahua custom when on raids, the warriors were on foot.

From early childhood Apache males trained as long-distance runners. Boys were routinely made to cover four-mile courses over rough country. On hot days they had to do it carrying a mouthful of water which they could neither swallow nor spit out. Gradually over the years, the distance was increased. By the time Apache males were full grown, they could travel 75 miles over scorched desert in a single day and be no worse the wear for their ordeal.

Clay Taggart was not yet the equal of his fellow renegades, but he could go farther on foot, and faster, than any white man in the territory. On this particular sunny day he loped at the head of the

Chiricahua, who were strung out in single file behind him. As was always the case when on the go,
no one spoke. The hardy warriors jogged in stoic
silence, their churning legs eating up the miles
with deceptive ease.

To the northwest, two days' travel by horseback,
was Fort Bowie. Together with Fort Apache, located farther north, the post was a bastion of
American military might in the southeast corner
of Arizona. Troopers out of Fort Bowie routinely
patrolled the border, so Clay was on the lookout
for them. He did not care to be taken by surprise,
as he had been after slaying the antelope.

Of the five members of the band, only Clay wore
a hat. Apaches, by and large, shunned headgear,
except for headbands of various colors. Clay's hat
was brown. It sported a wide brim that shaded his
eyes from the sun. Weeks ago, for the sheer hell
of it, Clay had stuck a feather in the crown.

Fiero often remarked that the hat looked ridiculous, but Clay refused to stop wearing it on raids.
It had become his trademark, serving to identify
him to any who might spot them.

Clay wanted to be recognized. He wanted those
who had ruined his life to know that he was very
much alive. He wanted them to quake with fear,
never knowing when he might show up on their
doorstep to exact vengeance for the wrongs they
had done him.

It was an hour before sunset when a telltale
plume of dust marked the position of the small
caravan. White Apache slowed, signaled to the
others, and veered into high rocks to the east of
the rutted track. He soon came within sight of the
wagons and riders.

Most were Mexicans, distinguished by their
sombreros and flared pants. Armed to the prover-

bial teeth, three riders were in front of the wagons, three behind. Bandoliers crisscrossed their chests. Double cartridge belts encircled their waists. Each man had two pistols in side holsters and a third wedged under the front of his belt. Each man carried either a Henry, a Spencer, or a Winchester. These were men who knew what they were doing. They would not be easy to take by surprise.

A pair of men rode on each of the last two wagons. One man handled the mule team while the other, bristling with hardware, kept watch.

White Apache was most interested in the lead wagon—and not because of the beefy, greasy half-breed armed with four pistols and a brass-frame Henry who was riding guard. His gaze was drawn to the long-haired driver, a Mexican woman who was dressed like a man and had a sawed-off shotgun propped between her legs.

Clay had heard of her. Anglos called her Sonora Sally. Mexicans knew her as *Hechicera Rojo*, the Red Witch. She was a wily smuggler who had been working the illicit border trade for the better part of a decade. Only once had she been caught, on the Mexican side. Saloon gossip had it that she had bribed her way out of jail and disappeared. Her men were all confirmed killers, *pistoleros* with no scruples. Rumor had it that she kept them in line by offering them shares in her operation, as well as letting them take turns sampling her feminine charms.

Every lawman in Arizona would have given their right arm for a crack at her. The army had posted circulars, asking anyone with information on her whereabouts to come forward.

But the White Apache had found her first. From a high roost he spied on them, debating what to

82

do. The wagons were bound to contain a lot of plunder. The big question was whether it was plunder the Apache could use, or whether they would be risking their lives for useless dry goods.

Then there was Sonora Sally to consider. Clay had an aversion to killing women, even a woman who made her living on the wrong side of the law. He attempted to come up with an excuse to let the smugglers go on their way unmolested.

The wagons rattled steadily southward. Now and then an outrider would go up to one of them and help himself to a dipper of water from a side-mounted barrel.

White Apache and the Chiricahua shadowed the smugglers until sunset. As the light dwindled, Sonora Sally guided her team into a gully; the others followed suit, and within no time they had a fire going and were treating themselves to coffee and beans.

When Clay was positive the gang had settled down for the night, he withdrew from his vantage point, silently signaling to the warriors as he did. They all joined him except for Ponce. The young warrior was left to keep watch.

Presently White Apache and the three Apache warriors were gathered under a rock overhang, squatting in a circle. Fiero spoke first. Simmering with excitement, he declared, "I say we attack before dawn. Most of the *Nakai-yes* will be asleep. We can kill half of them before the rest know what is happening. It will be easy."

"You always want to attack," White Apache pointed out, eliciting a grin from Cuchillo Negro. "But we must ask ourselves whether it would be worth it. What do we stand to gain?"

"Rifles, ammunition, horses," Fiero ticked them off.

"We have enough horses. We have plenty of guns from previous raids. And we have collected enough ammunition for an army." White Apache held his ground.

The hothead did not like it when someone disputed him. "So? Are you becoming lazy, *Lickoyee-shis-inday*? Since when is a warrior content with what he has? Have you forgotten that we are Apache? The *Shis-Inday* are warriors, before all else. We have always been so. We will always be so. My father, his father, and my father's father all lived by their quickness and their wits. We must do the same."

It was a valid point that White Apache could not dispute, so he did not even try. It would have done no good, anyway. Once Fiero made up his mind, changing it was like changing the course of a river—next to impossible unless you were the Almighty. He turned to Delgadito for support. "What do you say?"

The renegade leader thought it folly to go up against so many guns. In the old days, before *Lickoyee-shis-inday* usurped his position, he would have dismissed it as too reckless. But he had been working on a plan to win back the trust of the other warriors, and to that end, he had to side with them against *Lickoyee-shis-inday* whenever possible. So he answered, "Fiero's thoughts are mine. We have been idle too long. If we do this the right way, we will not lose anyone."

"And you?" White Apache asked Black Knife.

Cuchillo Negro had always been the most cautious member of the band. He always counseled against doing anything rash. This time was no different. "I once heard Cochise say that a wise warrior knows when to fight, and when not to. There is little to gain by attacking these *Nakai-yes*. I say we keep hunting. Something better will come along."

The wrangling would have gone on indefinitely had Ponce not materialized out of the shadows. "Come quickly," the young warrior urged.

"What has happened?" White Apache asked.

"You must see for yourselves."

Into the darkness they melted, spectral figures who made no more noise than real ghosts would. Invisible to the smugglers below, they laid flat along the gully rim.

Clay was taken aback to see that a girl of 10 or 12 had joined the smugglers. It was an Indian girl, of all people, clothed in a store-bought dress, the cheap kind sold at trading posts. He was going to ask Ponce where she had come from when she rose from near the fire and hobbled over to Sonora Sally and several *pistoleros*. Around her ankles were shackles. The chain was so short, she could not take full strides without falling on her face.

"She is a Mimbre," Fiero said.

White Apache did not know how the warrior could tell, but he took Fiero's word for it. All four of the warriors had keener eyesight than he did. At times, he had to marvel at their ability to distinguish objects so far off that he was hard-pressed to make the objects out.

Of the various Apache tribes, the Mimbres were more closely allied with the Chiricahua than any other. In part, it stemmed from the deep personal friendship Cochise had shared with Mangus Colorado, the former head of the Mimbres. In part, too, because the two tribes lived close to one another, so close that the borders of their recognized territories overlapped.

The girl in the gully was carrying a tin cup of coffee. She bent to hand it to Sonora Sally, and tripped. The hot brew splashed on the smuggler's neck. Sally shot to her feet with a howl, cuffed the girl so hard that she fell onto her side, then lustily cursed the child in Spanish.

White Apache sensed a change come over his companions. Not one moved. Not one uttered a sound. Yet they were different. Their forms gave the illusion of being chiseled in stone, as if they had tensed from head to toe. They were human panthers, anxious to rip and rend.

Sonora Sally stopped swearing and stomped to a wagon. From it she pulled what appeared to be a coil of rope. A sharp flick of her arm revealed the truth. A bullwhip unfurled with a crack, inches from the prone Mimbre. The girl crawled backward to get out of reach, but hampered by the leg irons she could not crawl fast enough. Sonora Sally stalked her. The whip arced again, its tip biting into the girl's shoulder, ripping the material and the soft flesh underneath.

"You will learn to be careful, savage!" the smuggler railed. "Or I will peel your hide piece by piece until there is nothing left."

Clay doubted the Indian girl understood. The child covered her face with her arms and rolled onto her stomach, but that did not stop the whip from raining down over and over, its searing tip cutting her arms, her legs, her feet. Blood trickled from the wounds, coating her wrists and lower legs.

The girl never let out a peep. Teeth clenched, she bore the torment with the fortitude of an Apache adult. When Sonora Sally finally tired and lowered her arm, the Mimbre brazenly sat up and stared defiantly at her. Two men promptly seized her.

Sally walked forward, coiling the whip. When

she was close enough, she swung, smashing the girl across the mouth with the heavy handle. The Mimbre was rocked by the blow. Another caused her knees to buckle. A third, delivered to her stomach, doubled her over, at which point the *pistoleros* let her drop.

Fiero's blood pulsed in his veins. It was all he could do to keep from charging down into the camp. "Now what do you say, *Lickoyee-shis-inday*?" he whispered.

White Apache did not have to say anything. They all knew what had to be done.

The girl lay still for the longest while, until Sonora Sally, or the Red Witch, as Clay was now inclined to think of her, walked over and kicked the Mimbre in the back. When the girl did not rise quickly enough to suit her, the Witch grabbed her by the hair and jerked her upright.

"That one is mine," Fiero whispered.

The captive was made to wait hand and foot on the men, serving them coffee, spreading out their blankets and doing other chores. She was poked, prodded and slapped. Through it all, she held her bloodied head high.

"If she were a little older, I would take her to be my woman," Ponce said.

The young warrior was the only member of the band who did not have a mate. The woman he had kidnapped from the *conducta* had later escaped. Shortly before that, a Chiricahua maiden for whom he cared, Firefly, had been brutally butchered by an army scout. Ponce was profoundly lonely but he would never let on as much.

White Apache slid back from the edge. Grunting to alert the others, he rose, but stayed low so the smugglers would not glimpse him. One by one, the Apache dogged his footsteps. When they were far enough from the gully to speak openly, he swung around and bluntly declared, "We will kill them all. It is agreed?"

"*Tats-an*," Fiero said vehemently.

"As for the *ish-tia-nay*, one of us must take her to her people when it is over," White Apache noted.

"*Shee-dah*," Ponce volunteered.

White Apache bent his neck to study the sky. Scattered pale clouds scuttled across the heavens, dominated by a sliver of moon. It would pose no problem to men trained from childhood to blend into the terrain as if they were part of it. "We must attack the *kunh-gan-hay* from both sides of the gully at once. Delgadito and Ponce from the east, the rest of us from the west."

Clay did not mention that he felt it best to have Fiero near him so he could keep an eye on the firebrand. The others would not do anything rash. Fiero—was Fiero.

"What will be the signal?" Delgadito posed the most important question.

"When you see me go over the rim."

Fiero grinned like a kid who had been granted his heart's desire. "At last, a battle! *Nah-kee-sah-tah* to *asht-lay*. I like those odds!"

12 to five? Only Fiero would, White Apache mused, as they soundlessly fanned out to take their positions. He returned to the same vantage point as before.

The smugglers were relaxing after their long day of arduous travel. Several played cards. Others had a game of dice going. The Red Witch huddled with a husky *pistolero* who could not keep his hands off her shapely body.

Left alone, the Mimbre squatted by the fire. She was the perfect picture of misery. But she did not cry; she did not so much as sniffle.

Clay admired the girl's grit. He scanned the smugglers again, seeking evidence of liquor. It would help immensely if some of the *pistoleros* were too drunk to offer much resistance, but evidently their boss kept them on a tight rein. Coffee was drunk in large quantities, but nothing else.

Shifting, White Apache sought sign of his companions. To the north, Ponce and Delgadito were working their way along the rim toward the far side. Fiero lay at the base of a boulder 30 feet away. Of Cuchillo Negro, no trace could be seen.

There was nothing else for Clay to do but wait. Crossing his arms, he rested his chin on a wrist and made himself comfortable.

The smugglers talked in low tones. Every so often one would laugh or curse. Toward midnight most of them turned in, sprawling out under the stars. The Mimbre girl was shoved into a wagon. The Red Witch and her husky friend entered another and vanished under a blanket. One man was left to stand guard. He roved the perimeter for a while, then tired and sat on a flat rock near the fire, warming his hands.

Time passed. The wagon into which the Red Witch and her admirer had gone commenced to squeak and jiggle, proving the rumors to be true. At least it was a common enough occurrence that the guard did not even look up and none of the sleepers awoke.

White Apache found himself growing drowsy sometime around two in the morning. He drew back from the edge and stood. Pacing, he shook his arms and turned his head back and forth to get his blood flowing.

Although Clay tried his utmost to emulate the Chiricahua, he could not yet go for days at a time without sleep, as they could. Delgadito had revealed that training along those lines started when Apache boys were about 10 years old. They would be encouraged to stay up later and later, until they could go a whole night without rest. Later, they would go two nights. It was all part of their everyday practice for when they would be old enough to go on raids. Clay had gone two nights once, and been so tired on the morning of the third day that he had slept fourteen straight hours without stirring. Delgadito had laughed, joking how Clay had the stamina of a five year old and needed the rest of a person over 80.

Of course, that had been back in the days when Clay and Delgadito were the best of friends. Or so Clay had believed until Cuchillo Negro secretly let him know that he was a pawn in Delgadito's grand scheme to regain a position of prominence in the tribe.

Since then, thanks to a series of quirks of fate, Clay had been the one who grew in influence while Delgadito's standing among his fellows had waned. Clay knew that Delgadito resented it. Every time one of the others looked to Clay for advice, Delgadito stewed.

By unspoken agreement, Clay Taggart now found himself the leader of the band. More and more, important decisions were left to him. It had been his idea, for instance, to steal women for wives. He had been the one to lead the last few raids, and no one had seen fit to object.

Not even Delgadito, which troubled Clay. The warrior was not one to stand by and do nothing while someone else usurped his position. Yet Delgadito had lifted neither his voice nor a finger in protest. It made Clay suspect that the crafty renegade was up to something, that Delgadito had a plan to turn the tables somewhere down the line. Probably when Clay least expected.

Clay shrugged. If it was meant to be, so be it. He had no choice but to go on with things as they were and hope to hell he did not wind up with cold steel buried between his ribs one dark night.

Unknown to the Chiricahua, Clay has his own plan. He had to keep the band together at all costs, so that one day soon he could launch a campaign of terror against those who had wronged him. Before it was over, Arizona soil would run red with the blood of his enemies.

More time went by. White Apache lay back down. By the position of the constellations he knew that dawn was approximately an hour off.

It was time.

There had been three changes of guard overnight. A wiry Mexican whose spurs jangled as he walked was at that moment making a circuit of the wagons and the stock. A Spencer slanted across his left shoulder, he whistled softly, not paying much attention to his surroundings.

Exactly as the White Apache had counted on. Holding the Winchester close to his side, he crept to the very brink. The unwary smuggler, shuffling slowly, passed beneath him and began to loop to the east.

White Apache went over the edge. Body flat, wriggling like an oversized serpent, he wormed onto the brush-littered slope and headed toward the bottom of the gully. He had to exercise the utmost care. The incline was littered with small stones, and in spots the earth itself was loose. Dislodging either would alert the man on guard.

A bush barred his path. White Apache made like an eel, slanting to the right to go around it. He paused to lift his head high enough to see the Mexican. The man had slowed and was searching in his pockets, possibly for the makings of a cigarette.

White Apache slid lower. He was so intent on not making any noise that he did not give much notice to the weeds to his right. If he had, he might have seen some of them quiver, as if to the passage of a slender form. If he had, he would not have been taken by surprise when a clump of stems unexpectedly parted and the blunt snout of a roving rattlesnake poked out.

Its forked tongue flicking, the deadly reptile slithered into the open, straight toward Clay Taggart.

Chapter Seven

William Randolph had tossed and turned most of the night. Sleeping outdoors, in his estimation, was a barbaric practice, fit for country bumpkins and simple savages, but certainly not for a man of culture and refinement. Lying on the ground was torture compared to the wonderfully soft king-size bed he customarily slept in back in New York.

Even having three blankets under him and two on top did not help. Each morning he got up to find bruises everywhere. His skin was just too delicate for him to live primitively for any length of time. Yet that was exactly what he had been doing for the better part of a week.

The reporter frowned and sat up. Since he couldn't sleep, he might as well rise and get a pot of coffee brewing. Sunrise could not be far off, and a piping hot cup of Arbuckle's would go a long way toward restoring his spirits.

Stretching, Randolph surveyed the camp. Ten

feet away slept the accursed woman, a blanket pulled clear up to her chin. In repose her features were angelic, almost beautiful, and for a moment he almost forgot all the trouble she had given him. Almost, but not quite.

Randolph smirked. Little did she know that he had outsmarted her, that her plea to Gov. Goodwin had been wasted effort. The governor's safe-conduct pass would not save her precious cousin now.

One of the three men hired in Tucson to accompany Randolph and Amelia was over by the horses, keeping watch. Smoke curled from a pipe in his mouth.

The reporter regarded the trio as typical border ruffians. Their clothes were largely unkempt, their chins coated with rough stubble. Their sole redeeming grace was Quid's assurance that all three were proficient gunmen and knew how to live off the land.

Randolph knelt next to the smoldering embers of their campfire and added fuel to rekindle it. He had to hand it to Benjamin Quid. The bounty hunter had proved to be as good as his word.

The day they met, across from the Park Theatre in Tucson, Randolph had sensed a kindred soul. Like him, Quid worshiped the almighty dollar. Like him, Quid would do anything to fill his pockets. And like him, Quid could be as devious as a fox when it came to getting his way.

Once Randolph had heard the bounty hunter's tale of being made a fool of by the White Apache, Randolph knew he had his man. He had made his pitch and been overjoyed when Quid readily agreed to a 60-40 split. Quid's partner, Plunkett, had complained that he thought their cut should be more until Randolph pointed out that he was the only one who could get Amelia to do as they wanted, and without her unwitting help, they had no means of luring Clay Taggart into a trap.

For over an hour that day, Randolph and the two bounty hunters had sat in a murky corner of the saloon, plotting. Quid had agreed to find several reliable men to accompany Amelia and him. Since the bounty hunter knew the region fairly well, Quid had also suggested an ideal spot for the ambush.

Now, after almost a week of travel, Randolph and Amelia were nearing that spot, a place known as Devil's Canyon situated deep in the Dragoon Mountains. Why it was called Devil's Canyon, no one seemed to know. The important thing was there was only one way in or out.

Quid and Plunkett and two men with them had been shadowing Randolph and Amelia since they left Tucson. The bounty hunters would lie in wait at the canyon mouth, and when Clay Taggart rode into their sights, they would cut him to ribbons in a hail of lead.

The White Apache would be gunned down before he could reach his cousin. Amelia would never get to give him the safe-conduct pass, so the bounty would still be in force when he was slain.

Randolph chuckled to himself. He had the plan worked out to the letter. Nothing could go wrong.

At that moment, the loud crackle of a branch catching flame brought Amelia Taggart out of a troubled sleep. She had been having a horrible dream in which Clay was being led up a gallows to a waiting noose. A huge throng ringed the scaffold. In a panic, she had tried to push through them to get to him, but no one would move aside to let her pass. His head had been stuck into the noose and the hangman had tightened it around his throat. Then, just as the hooded figure was about to throw the lever that would drop the trap door and send Clay to his doom, her cousin had looked up, gazed smack into her eyes and asked sadly, "How could you, Amelia? How could you?"

Amelia had long believed that dreams were important. Some were windows to a person's innermost thoughts; others were omens of things to come. Whichever the case in this instance, his question haunted her as she rose and ran a hand through her tangled hair.

Randolph had not yet noticed her. He was grinning, as if at a secret joke.

It puzzled Amelia. He had been acting strangely ever since her visit with the governor. For a while he had been in a funk, hardly speaking unless spoken to, giving her the impression that she had done something wrong.

On reaching Tucson, the newsman's attitude had changed again. Suddenly he had been all smiles, as considerate as could be.

Amelia did not know what to make of his peculiar behavior. Her intuition warned that he was up to something, yet what it might be eluded her.

Had the dream been an omen in that regard? Amelia pondered. Or was it a reflection on her efforts? Gov. Goodwin had promised to do all in his power to ensure Clay spent the rest of his life in prison instead of being hanged, but maybe the governor's influence would do no good. Maybe Clay would go to the gallows, and it would all be her fault.

Amelia walked past the two gunmen who were still asleep. "Good morning, Mr. Randolph," she said softly, so as not to awaken them.

Randolph was so startled, he jumped. Sheepishly, he replied, "Good morning to you, Miss Taggart. I trust you slept well?"

"Not really, no."

"It's the excitement of soon seeing your cousin again after so many years," Randolph said. "Just think. By this time tomorrow we'll be at Devil's Canyon. Then all we have to do is make camp and wait for Clay to show up."

In a leather case beside Amelia's saddle were the circulars her benefactor had made up before they left Tucson. Amelia regarded it thoughtfully. "Do you really think it will work? What if he doesn't see them?"

Randolph added a handful of twigs to the growing flames. "I've been assured that word of mouth spreads news fast in this region. Sooner or later your cousin will learn of your whereabouts. He'll come. Trust me."

"But what if it's too late? What if we've left?"

Randolph humored her. "My dear, we have enough provisions to last us a month, which is more than enough time." He stared at the man smoking a pipe. "My only worry is that your cousin might not come alone. Mr. Stirco and his friends are fine shots, but there are only three of them."

"Clay would never let me come to any harm. And I won't let him or his Apache friends hurt you, not after all you've done on his behalf."

"How sweet of you," Randolph said, amused by the delicious irony. Upending the dregs in the coffeepot, he made for the shallow stream they had been following for the past two days.

A pink tinge adorned the eastern horizon, and somewhere far off birds were chirping.

Randolph had to concede a certain humble charm to the wilderness. The stark mountains, the vista of rolling slopes and gorges and ravines, had a crudely majestic air about them. In a limited way, so did the sea of boulders and sand and blistered earth. When he got home, he would tell all his friends that Arizona was an interesting place to visit, but no one in their right mind would ever want to live there.

Amelia sat on a log to warm herself. The other gunmen were stirring. Soon they would be on their way again, another day spent in the saddle under the broiling sun. She didn't mind. She was growing to love this rugged land with its crags and buttes and mesas, with its beautiful canyons, its picturesque chaparral, its forests of stately ponderosa pines. Arizona Territory stirred her soul as Ohio and Missouri never had. It helped her to understand why her cousin had stayed.

If only he hadn't turned renegade.

What could he possibly hope to gain, other than an early grave?

Clay Taggart might have been inclined to agree. He froze as the sidewinder slithered toward him. Suddenly it coiled and reared, its head less than two feet from his neck. He held himself still as the snake swayed and rattled its tail.

The Mexican on guard heard. Spinning, the man leveled his rifle and cocked his head, attempting to pinpoint exactly where the sound came from.

Out of the corner of an eye, White Apache watched the rattlesnake. He tensed his arms to roll aside if it came at him even though his reflexes were no match for the reptile's flashing speed. Its tongue darted in his direction, again and again. Its tail rose, rattling louder. He could see the tips of its fangs through its parted lips.

White Apache also saw the guard coming toward the west slope. It wouldn't take the man long to notice him, lying in an open spot as he was. He had to crawl into the weeds, but any movement, however slight, might provoke the rattlesnake into attacking.

The sidewinder slid closer. Moving slowly, almost hypnotically, it lowered its head and crawled to within inches of Clay's throat, which was no more than a hand's width above the ground. It stopped rattling.

Clay's skin prickled. He broke out in a cold sweat. A bite in the arm or the leg he could deal with, and possibly survive. No one, though, ever lived after being bitten in the neck. The venom would reach his heart in seconds. Paralysis would set in within the first minute. Within three, he would be in convulsions. Within five, he would be dead.

The guard, almost at the bottom, was scouring the slope, lower down.

White Apache lost sight of the sidewinder's head. He felt something tickle his throat, and moments later the head appeared on his right side, moving slowly away. The snake brushed him several times. In each instance he erupted in goose bumps. Soon the tail slid out from under him, but he stayed where he was until the rattler entered a patch of dry brush.

None too soon.

The Mexican had started to climb. He was slightly north of White Apache's position, slinking toward a rock outcropping.

Drawing his Bowie, White Apache angled to intercept the man. A silent kill was called for. And a swift one. There was no telling how soon the other smugglers would wake up.

Abruptly, the guard halted and pivoted.

White Apache was screened by sparse brush. In broad daylight he would have been spotted. At night, shrouded in shadow, he was safe. Or so he thought until the Mexican hiked the Spencer and peered right at him. Quickly, he reversed his grip on the Bowie so that he held it by the flat of the blade. The guard took a stride. Then another.

Higher up, a pebble rattled.

Instinctively, the Mexican swung toward the sound, and as he did, White Apache reared onto his knees, flung back his right arm and hurled the heavy Bowie with all the skill and strength at his command.

The range was only 10 feet. The big knife was a blur. Flying end over end, it reached the guard as the man turned back. There was a spongy *thunk*. The Bowie sliced through the man's shirt and flesh, sinking to the hilt. A gurgle of shock burst from the Mexican, who dropped the Spencer, grabbed the knife and pulled. The knife came partway out, no more. Blood gushed as the guard staggered, opening his mouth to warn his friends.

White Apache shot to his feet and sprinted toward the man to shut him up. It was hopeless, though. He could never reach him in time.

Someone else did. A brawny arm looped around the guard's neck from the rear. A long butcher knife speared into his ribs three times in swift succession. At the last stroke, the Mexican gave up the ghost, crumpling in a miserable heap.

Fiero, bloody knife in hand, grinned broadly at White Apache. The warrior was in his element. He lived for the intoxicating thrill of combat, for the tingling joy that slaying enemies brought him. Even by Chiricahua standards, Fiero was bloodthirsty. He would be the first to admit as much. He would also admit that he liked being the way

100

he was, and he had no intention of ever changing.

White Apache rushed over to reclaim the Bowie. Fiero said nothing, just melted into the grass. In moments White Apache was doing the same. He glided rapidly to the gully floor, verified that none of the horses or mules had caught the scent of fresh blood, then scrambled under the nearest wagon. It happened to be the same one the Red Witch and her lover had climbed into.

Some of the smugglers were snoring. Others slept quietly, blissfully ignorant of the bronzed death descending upon them.

White Apache, Bowie in hand, crawled to the inner wheel. Beyond it lay a half-breed, one arm crooked over his face. Setting down the Winchester, White Apache inched around the wheel's rim. He was almost close enough for a killing stroke when the breed's arm moved.

The man was awake. He saw White Apache. From his mouth ripped the terrified cry, "Apache! Apache! *Cuidado, amigos! Cuidado!*"

All hell broke loose. Smugglers sprang from their blankets, some fumbling for rifles, others drawing pistols. The half-breed pushed erect but only got to one knee before White Apache was on him. A revolver glinted. It went off almost in White Apache's ear as the Bowie lanced into the cutthroat's abdomen above the belt. The man gasped, grunted, and folded over.

White Apache drew back the Bowie to finish his victim off, but suddenly guns were firing all over the place. Slugs smashed into the wagon, into the spokes of the wheel, into the ground around him. Diving under the wagon, he snatched the Winchester on the fly and rolled out the other side as war whoops rent the air.

Dashing to the front of the wagon, White

Apache drew abreast of the seat just as the husky *pistolero* emerged. The man's shirt was missing, his pants half buttoned. He held a nickel-plated Remington, but he was looking toward the center of the camp, not down at his very feet.

White Apache slanted the Winchester and stroked the trigger. The .44-40 boomed and bucked, the slug catching the smuggler low in the torso. The impact flung the man from the wagon and he hit the ground hard, headfirst.

In the wagon a pistol cracked. A bullet bit into the seat so close to White Apache's face that flying slivers stung his cheek. He ducked, responded in kind. Working the lever of his rifle, he raced toward the next wagon, the one containing the Mimbre girl.

Ponce beat him there. The young warrior materialized out of nowhere, vaulted onto the seat and ducked under the canvas cover. In moments he reappeared, the girl held close to his chest. As he stepped to the end of the seat and coiled to jump, a smuggler raced up with a sawed-off Loomis shotgun. At that range, the scattergun would blow holes the size of melons in the pair.

White Apache was not about to let that happen. Snapping a shot from the waist, he hit the smuggler above the ear. The powerful .44-40 slug exploded out the other side of the man's cranium, showering brains, blood and bits of bone over the ground. The shotgun went off, but into the wagon, not into the warrior and the maiden.

Ponce acknowledged their being spared with a nod. In a lithe bound he gained the sanctuary of the darkness and vanished into it, taking the girl to safety.

Elsewhere, the raging clash had reached a crescendo. Guns blasted nonstop. Men swore in Spanish and in English. Some screamed. A stricken man wailed like a banshee. Six of the smugglers were down. The rest had sought cover under or behind wagons.

White Apache sprang for the wagon in front of him as rounds peppered the ground and leaden hornets buzzed through the air. Gaining momentary safety, he crouched, then peeked out. He saw one of the Mexicans slinking toward the panicked, milling horses and went to take a shot, but the man sank from sight in some high weeds.

Suddenly there was a lull as both sides reloaded. In the all too brief silence, White Apache could hear ringing in his ears. And one thing more. From the wagon which held the Red Witch came a faint ripping noise. A knife blade had been shoved through the canvas. As the gunfire resumed, the canvas parted. Out poked the head of the Red Witch. In a twinkling, she was wriggling through the opening she had made.

White Apache raised the Winchester. He had her dead to rights, but as he fixed a bead on her chest, a dusky figure appeared for a heartbeat in the brush near her wagon. It was a figure he recognized. Lowering the rifle, he let her slip to the ground and flee up the gully. She was almost out of sight when Fiero rose from concealment, knife in hand, and cat footed after her.

Turning his attention back to the smugglers, White Apache saw one go down with a neat hole in the center of his chest. The shot had come from the east rim, from Delgadito. White Apache added his rifle to the fray and winged a man crouched behind a wheel.

Off to the left, in a cluster of boulders, another rifle cracked. That had to be Cuchillo Negro, White Apache knew. Between the three of them, they had the smugglers pinned down in a cross fire. Since he doubted the Mexicans were willing to stay where they were and be picked off one by one, he foresaw them making a break for the horses at any moment.

It came seconds later. At a yip from a burly man in a sombrero, those smugglers able to do so surged to their feet and dashed toward their stock. They fired as rapidly as they could work their rifles, and in no time a wreath of gunsmoke engulfed them, concealing them as effectively as a thick fog.

White Apache spied a pair of legs, aimed twelve inches above them and fired twice. A body dropped, the smuggler twitching and kicking.

Delgadito and Cuchillo Negro were also pouring fire into the gunsmoke. Flashes from within it testified to the wild shooting of the Mexicans.

A horse whinnied in agony. Then a second. White Apache realized the Chiricahua were to blame. As a former rancher, as a man who had been raised around horses and thought more highly of them than he did of most people, he was appalled that they should needlessly suffer. But there was nothing he could do about it. The Apache were not about to stop firing so long as a single enemy stood. Also, to them a horse was just a horse. They harbored no sentimental feelings toward any animal.

Hooves drummed. A man riding bareback galloped out of the gunsmoke, leaning low over his mount's neck, a smoking pistol in his left hand. He fired at the rim, trying to keep Delgadito pinned down so he could make his escape.

Delgadito was not to be denied. His hatred of the *Nakai-yes* would not allow him to let a single one get away. It had been Sonoran bounty hunters who had massacred his wife, relatives and friends. All those he cared for, all those who had looked up to him as their leader, all those who had relied on him to keep them safe, had been exterminated like rabid dogs by ruthless Mexican butchers.

So it was no small wonder Delgadito risked exposing himself so he would have a clearer shot at the fleeing rider. He tracked the rolling gait of the man's bay, adjusted his aim accordingly, and snapped off a shot when the Mexican was almost out of sight. The smuggler flung his arms out, pitched backward and crashed into mesquite.

White Apache noticed that no more shots came from the boulders where Cuchillo Negro had been concealed, and he worried that something had happened to his friend. He started to back up and go around the wagon when a wounded smuggler across the clearing rose on one knee and snapped a shot at him. White Apache ducked as the lead bit into the wood above him. Thinking to return the favor, he straightened.

But the smuggler was already being taken care of. Like a panther out of the night, Cuchillo Negro pounced, bearing the man to the earth. A black-handled knife flashed once, twice, three times. Then, as swiftly as he had struck, Cuchillo Negro melted into the darkness again.

Five smugglers were still alive. Two, both severely wounded, were under the farthest wagon. The rest were among the prancing horses, striving desperately to climb on and get out of there.

White Apache left the sanctuary of the wagon bed, circling to the right to get closer to the men trying to ride off. The wounded ones were not going anywhere and could be finished off at the band's leisure. He passed the wagon the Red Witch had been in, paused and sought a target.

Before he could stroke the trigger, a steely hand clamped on his left ankle, and his leg was yanked out from under him, toppling him onto his back.

It was the half-breed White Apache had stabbed in the abdomen, a man White Apache assumed to be dead. Very much alive, on his knees next to the wagon tongue, his shirt and hands coated with blood, the man swept a dagger on high and closed in for the kill.

Chapter Eight

White Apache's rifle was across his chest. He did not have time to point it and fire. Instead he lashed the stock at the smuggler's head. He missed, but he thwarted the man's initial attempt to stab him. Flinging himself to the left, he heard the knife thud into the dirt. White Apache pushed to his knees as the breed came at him a third time. In the nick of time he blocked a swing that would have imbedded the dagger in his neck. He drove the rifle barrel into the man's gut. It doubled the smuggler over, but before White Apache could press his advantage, the man grasped the Winchester and threw all his weight into shoving White Apache onto the ground.

Locked together, they grappled. White Apache had to let go of his rifle to seize the breed's knife arm as it swept toward him. The tip of the blade was inches from his left eye. He strained to throw the smuggler off, but failed. Desperation lent the man inhuman brawn. Just keeping the knife at bay took every bit of might White Apache possessed. The smuggler, his lips curled, growled like a wild beast.

They rolled to the right. They rolled to the left. White Apache rammed a knee into the other's crotch but it did not have an effect. The smuggler tried the same with him. Twisting, White Apache bore the brunt on his thigh. Exquisite pain racked him, and for a moment he thought he would lose his grip on his foe's wrist and be stabbed. Firming his hold, he struggled to his knees, pulling the man up with him.

They were in the open now, and one of the men under the wagon across the clearing took a shot at White Apache. The zing of the slug galvanized him into a lunge to his left, onto his shoulder.

In a deft move, the half-breed shifted his weight and executed a partial flip so that he wound up on top. Using both arms, he threw everything he had into a supreme effort to bury his slim blade.

The tip edged toward White Apache's face. His muscles bulged with effort but he could not hold the blade back. He felt the razor point prick his cheek, felt a tiny trickle of blood. Suddenly arching his legs up and around, White Apache locked his ankles around the breed's thick neck, then wrenched his hips to one side.

It worked. The smuggler was flung to the dirt. He rose quickly, though, even though his exertion was causing his stomach wound to bleed more profusely than ever. Most men would have keeled over long ago. But not this one. He was as tough as rawhide, as vicious as a loco wolf.

White Apache dodged a thrust to the chest, swiveled and evaded a slash at his throat. Hurling himself to the rear to gain room to move, he drew the Colt as he landed flat. His thumb jerked the hammer and he fired his first shot as the smuggler reared, fired his second as the smuggler lunged, fired his third when the man was so close that he could see beads of sweat on the breed's brow and fired his fourth and final shot with his barrel pressed against the cutthroat's chest. The man collapsed on top of him.

White Apache exhaled and tossed the body off. Staying low, he reloaded the pistol, his fingers flying. Holstering it, he snaked to his rifle.

The fight was winding down. Only one of the wounded men under the wagon still lived. Over at the horses, two men were on their feet but one limped badly. A number of horses had broken loose and run off. Those that remained continued to mill every which way, neighing stridently all the while, raising a cloud of dust which mingled with the gun smoke to form a choking layer that blinded smugglers and mounts alike.

White Apache caught sight of Delgadito working his way down from the rim toward the animals and turned to concentrate on the smuggler under the opposite wagon. The man was on his belly behind the body of his fallen *amigo*, reloading a Spencer. White Apache could not get a clear shot.

Dashing to the right, into the brush, White Apache hunkered and surveyed the campsite to ensure no others were alive. He wanted no more nasty surprises like the half-breed. Other than a convulsing Mexican, none of the prone forms moved. Satisfied, he stalked the wounded man, using patches of weed and brush to his advantage. In the process he drew near the horses, but he counted on the last two smugglers being too busy trying to catch a horse to spot him.

The smuggler with the Spencer suddenly crawled to the north, staying under the middle of the wagon bed where it was darkest.

If White Apache had stayed by the Red Witch's wagon, he would have had a perfect shot. As it was, one of the wheels and the dead man's legs blocked his view.

Among the horses and mules, a Mexican fell. The other one gave up striving to mount and fled on foot.

Delgadito gave chase.

That freed White Apache to rise and sprint toward the wagon that shielded the last of their adversaries. It seemed lunacy, rushing into the open, but there was a method to his apparent madness. On the run, he jumped up and caught hold of the top of the rear loading gate as a shot blistered the fringe on his left moccasin. Springing up and over, he landed atop a pile of long crates that filled the bed.

Under the wagon, the smuggler cursed.

White Apache moved toward the front. He hoped to do so without being detected but the boards under the crates squeaked. Stopping in the center, he pulled the Bowie and quickly slashed the canvas on both sides. Now all he had to do was wait. Eventually the smuggler would attempt to sneak off, and he would be ready.

Resting on his knees, White Apache sheathed the knife, then pried the slit on the right open. Nothing moved. He did the same on the left. The cutthroat was not there. Nor was there any movement to the front or the back. The man still had to be underneath the wagon.

Somewhere down the gully a rifle boomed. A revolver cracked twice in reply. Again the rifle blasted, and this time it was punctuated by a short

110

shriek which faded to a gurgling whine.

Delgadito, White Apache figured, had caught up with the man who had fled on foot. He pressed an eye to the right-hand slit once more. Then to the left-hand opening. Nothing. The smuggler under the wagon was taking his sweet time. White Apache wondered if the man was too weak from his wound to run for it.

Then there was a thump, as if something had bumped the bottom of the bed. White Apache peeked out the right-hand cut and saw the Mexican heading north, up the gully. One of the smuggler's shoulders drooped at an unnatural angle, suggesting his collar bone had been shattered. But that did not impair his legs, and he bounded like a terrified jackrabbit for the safety of the same boulders Cuchillo Negro had hidden behind a short while ago.

Sticking the Winchester's muzzle through the rent, White Apache fixed a hasty bead and fired. At the selfsame instant, another rifle thundered. Twin slugs slammed into the cutthroat's back. The smuggler hurtled forward as if swatted by a giant invisible hand and smashed onto his stomach near one of the boulders. His arms waving feebly, he grabbed hold of it and laboriously pulled himself to his knees. As he tried to rise higher, the other rifle cracked once more. The smuggler sank onto his belly, leaving a wide crimson smear on the boulder.

White Apache moved to the front of the wagon. Cuchillo Negro was 10 feet away, adding cartridges to his rifle. The warrior noticed him and nodded.

"*Yusn* was with us, *Lickoyee-shis-inday.*"

To the east, the sky was brightening rapidly. Soon the sun would appear. White Apache went

111

to climb down, then thought better of the idea. Moving to the crates, he carefully pried at the top of one with his Bowie until he had a crack wide enough to expose the contents. Inside were Spencer carbines, new models in perfect condition. Based on the number of crates, White Apache calculated there were enough to arm a small army. It spawned an idea, which for the time being he kept to himself.

Delgadito was approaching as White Apache emerged. Delgadito nodded once, curtly, then held out the gun belt and pistol that had belonged to the smuggler he had slain. "We will have no shortage of guns now," he said.

"Your words are more true than you imagine." White Apache indicated the wagon. "Look in there."

As Delgadito went to comply, a piercing whoop split the crisp morning air. Strolling toward them was Fiero. The firebrand had painted his cheeks, forehead and chest with bands of bright, fresh blood. An arrogant grin plastered his face as he came to a halt and extended his left hand for them to see the object he held. "I made her eat her own breasts before I was done."

It was the Red Witch's scalp, blood dripping from the thin strip of flesh to which the hair was attached. White Apache was surprised. Unlike Indians who lived on the Plains, Apache rarely took scalps. They did not decorate their lodges with such grisly trophies or adorn coup sticks with them, as was the custom among the Sioux and Cheyenne.

"What do you plan to do with it?" White Apache asked.

"I will give it to the Mimbre so she will have

something to remember this day by. Where is she?"

Just then, Ponce and the girl came around the northernmost wagon. He still carried her, her head resting on his shoulder. "We are here," he announced, accenting the "we."

White Apache crossed to meet them. "How badly is she hurt?"

"See for yourself."

The young warrior gently set the girl down. Up close, her bruises and welts were legion. A score of cuts from the whip marked her body. Dried blood caked her in spots.

White Apache saw that he had been mistaken. She was older than he had thought, perhaps fifteen or sixteen, but small for her age. Her doe eyes fixed on Ponce and would not leave his face.

Fiero came over. "Here girl," he said gruffly. "When you hear someone say that the *Shis-Inday* can be friends with the *Nakai-yes* or the white-eyes, hold this. It will remind you of how wrong they are."

Without looking directly at him, the girl took the gift. "Thank you," she said softly.

"Do you have a name?" Fiero inquired.

"*Nah-tanh.*"

It meant Corn Flower. For the girl to have her own name was unique. Long ago White Apache had learned that many Apache women did not. They were known simple as *ish-tai-nay*, or woman.

Fiero studied her. "You are brave for your age, *Nah-tanh*. You should have a man who is just as brave, or more so." He thumped on his chest. "I am that man. Among the Chiricahua, none have more courage. Ask any of my people." Fiero held himself straight and proud. "I offer you the honor of being my woman. I already have one, but I am a good hunter, a fine provider. You will never go hungry, never want for clothes. What do you say?"

Clay Taggart could scarcely believe his ears. The hapless girl had been through sheer hell. She was battered and bloody and weak. She was on the brink of exhaustion, alone among strangers, many miles from her family, her home. Yet the firebrand had the raw nerve to ask her to be his mate. Clay didn't like it one bit.

Neither did Ponce. The young warrior stepped protectively in front of her, planting his legs wide. "If she wants a man, she should take someone closer to her age," he boldly declared.

Fiero did not bat an eye. "What does age have to do with it? I am strong; I am healthy, and I know how to please women. She should be flattered that I give her the chance to share my wickiup."

Everyone there could tell that Ponce was about to say something Fiero would resent. White Apache grew alarmed. An insulted warrior had the right to issue a formal challenge, and should Fiero see fit to do so, the band would be shy one young warrior in very short order.

Moving up to Ponce before he could speak, White Apache put a friendly hand on the warrior's shoulder and said, "Corn Flower has had a very rough time. She can give Fiero an answer after she rests. Find a quiet spot where she can sleep undisturbed."

No warrior ever had to take an order from another. Every Apache was his own free man, to do as he pleased when he pleased. Ponce could have refused. He could have made an issue of Fiero's offer. He certainly wanted to. About to push *Lickoyee-shis-inday* aside, something about the

114

look White Apache gave him, stopped him. Glancing at Cuchillo Negro, he saw the same look. The magnitude of the mistake he had been about to make slowly dawned. "I will do as you want, White Apache," he said, gratefully.

Clay turned to Fiero, afraid the hothead would insist Corn Flower decide right that moment. To his relief, the temperamental warrior moved toward the littered bodies, saying, "I am going to skin one of them."

"Skin one?" White Apache said, shocked. The renegades were guilty of many atrocities, but never before had one taken off the hide of another. "Why would you want to do such a thing?"

"I got the idea from a Comanche I killed many winters ago," Fiero explained, bending to examine a thickset Mexican. "He had a pouch made from human skin. I was young and did not think to keep it." He ripped the smuggler's shirt, then rolled the corpse over and poked the dead man's back. "I was stupid. It was a fine pouch, and I have wanted one like it ever since."

"Help yourself," White Apache said, for want of anything better to say. The notion repulsed him, but not as much as it should have—which bothered him a little. It seemed that the longer he stayed with the renegades, the less the constant brutality upset him. Acts that once would have churned his stomach, he now took in stride.

Before a golden crown rimmed the horizon, the smugglers had been stripped of their weapons. The rifles, revolvers, derringers, knives, daggers and dirks were piled in the wagon containing the Spencers. In the other wagons White Apache found ordinary trade goods, including a score of thick blankets the women would like.

Delgadito and Cuchillo Negro rounded up as

many horses and mules as they could find: 18, all tolled. Ropes were looped around the necks of each to form a long string.

Fiero peeled a large square of skin off the back of a half-breed. Going to a horse accidentally shot during the battle, he cracked its skull with a heavy boulder. From the cranial cavity he extracted the brains, scooping them out with his hand. These he rubbed onto both sides of the skin to keep it soft and supple until he was ready to fashion his pouch.

Treating hides with brains was a common Indian practice. Women belonging to certain Plains tribes simmered brains in water to dissolve them to the consistency of a thin paste, then rubbed the paste onto pelts.

White Apache made coffee. The warriors gathered around. A dispute broke out over whether to hide the Spencers and other weapons somewhere nearby and come back for them later or whether to head for their sanctuary in the Dragoons right away. Fiero wanted to go on raiding. But White Apache, Cuchillo Negro and Delgadito insisted it was wiser to take their plunder while they could. Reluctantly, Fiero agreed.

That left the matter of the Mimbre. Ponce had been absent the whole time, so he was not there to hear Fiero say, "It will be nice to have a strong girl like her to do my cooking and sewing. She will last many years."

Cuchillo Negro was about to take a swallow, but stopped. "You count your horses before they are stolen. Maybe she will not want to live with you."

"What woman would not?"

White Apache smothered a laugh by pretending to cough. In all his born days, he had never met anyone so outright cocksure as Fiero. Then a sobering thought hit him, and the mirth promptly died. He was wrong. He did know someone as smug, someone even more cruelly arrogant.

Miles Gillett, the man who had stolen Clay's woman and his land, was a lot like Fiero. Both men did as they damn well wanted without any regard for the feelings of others. But where Fiero assumed his belligerence by virtue of his very nature, Miles Gillett cultivated being vicious as some people might cultivate the social graces. Gillett worked at it day and night.

Clay had never liked the man, from the very first day they met. Right away he'd recognized that Gillett believed himself to be superior to everyone else. The man treated one and all with cold disdain. And when he wanted something, he had no qualms whatsoever about crushing anyone who stood in his way.

Some men craved power like others craved liquor or sweets. They could not get enough of it. Miles Gillett, one of the wealthiest ranchers in the entire territory, with one of the biggest spreads west of the Mississippi, was never satisfied with what he had. He always craved more, more, more.

Clay often wondered how many other men Gillett had ruined over the years. There must have been dozens, yet Gillett had never been caught doing anything illegal. With his money and influence, Gillett could always cover his tracks. In Clay's case, Gillett had set him up as a murderer, then sicced the long arm of the law on him to finish him off. All nice and legal-like.

Gillett was pure evil, through and through. He liked to squash people as if they were bugs. There was no reasoning with him, no convincing him

that any course other than the one he had picked
was the right one.

The only way to stop a man like that, Clay
mused, was to kill him. Staring at the wagon that
contained the Spencers, Clay realized that fate
had played into his hands. If things went as he
wanted, within a year Miles Gillett and all those
who had done him wrong would be pushing up
grama grass.

The voices of his companions brought an end
to White Apache's reverie. Taking a sip of coffee,
he listened to Cuchillo Negro address Fiero.

"We have been friends for many winters, have
we not?"

"This is so," Fiero answered.

"Our arrows have flown side by side toward our
enemies, have they not?"

Furrows lined Fiero's forehead. He had never
been a deep thinker and he did not like it when
other men tried to tie him up in knots of words.
Unsure of the point Black Knife was trying to
make, he became wary. "Yes."

"We have hunted together, feasted together,
drank *twilt-kah-yee* together."

"Yes, yes," Fiero said impatiently. "So?"

"So it would sadden me if my brother were not
able to accept the decision the *ninya* is going to
make."

Fiero still did not see the point. "Can my brother
see into her mind that he knows what she will say
before she says it?"

Cuchillo Negro was slow to answer. As always
when dealing with Fiero, words had to be most
carefully chosen. "The minds of women are
closed to men. That is why women are one of
the great mysteries of life." He paused. "But a
man can learn to read the trail of a woman's

118

thoughts much as he reads the trail of an animal he hunts. The words they say, the looks they give, the way they hold their bodies, it can tell a man many things."

"And you think the *ish-tia-nay* will not want to share my wickiup?"

"I know she will not."

Fiero gave a toss of his shoulder. "So be it. Does my brother think so little of me that he imagines I would grow upset over something a female does?"

"My brother must admit that he is always ready to stand up for what he believes to be his. *Gian-nah-tah.*"

"If the girl is not smart enough to know a good thing when it is offered to her, I will not object."

"Even if she decides that she wants someone else instead of you?"

"Who could she—" Fiero began, then stopped, the answer coming to him in a flash of insight. He remembered how the *ninya* had rested her head on Ponce's shoulder, how Ponce had hovered over the virgin as if she were something precious to him. He saw the others staring at him, saw the troubled expression *Lickoyee-shis-inday* wore, and discerned the truth. They were worried he would slay Ponce over the girl.

Inwardly, Fiero was amused. Sometimes his fellow warriors were like women themselves, getting upset over things over which they had no control. A warrior had the right to issue a formal challenge whenever he felt he had been slighted by another. But in this case Ponce had done nothing to merit it. And in any event, he was not about to stoop so low as to fight over a woman. "Let the *ninya* decide as she wishes. It is of no concern to me."

White Apache was relieved. Thanks to Cuchillo Negro, an explosive situation had been defused. Their next order of business was to get the Spencers and the stolen stock to their safe haven.

They headed out at noon, White Apache handling the wagon. The Chiricahua were all on horseback. Cuchillo Negro and Delgadito roved far ahead, on the lookout for cavalry patrols or other threats. Fiero rode well to the rear to keep an eye on their back trail. The string of extra horses and mules were left in the care of Ponce and Corn Flower.

For four uneventful days the renegades forged steadily northward. Twice they saw smoke from campfires in the distance and made wide detours to avoid being seen. Presently they reached the Tucson-Mesilla road. It was late in the afternoon.

White Apache did want to cross in broad daylight since the road was heavily traveled. Hidden in a dry wash a few hundred yards to the south, he sat in the shade of the wagon with Ponce and the girl and waited for the sun to go down.

Delgadito appeared, riding slowly, something clutched in his left hand. "Cuchillo Negro keeps watch," he said in thickly accented English. Of the four Chiricahua, he was the only one who spoke the white man's tongue. He had a long way to go before he would be fluent, and he practiced every chance he got. "A few white-eyes go by. No bluecoats." Holding out the item he held, he asked, "What does the talking paper say?"

White Apache stood. It was a circular. Quite often the band came on similar small posters, either tacked to trees along roads or placed at springs and other stopover points where travelers were bound to see them. Many were about him, about the bounty on his head, or else warnings to be on the lookout for his band.

Clay took one look at this one and felt his innards turn to ice.

Chapter Nine

"Why the hell do we have to go so damn slow?" Travis Belcher wanted to know. "I swear to God, this heat is killing me."

Benjamin Quid shifted in the saddle to fix the young gun shark with a withering look. "The heat will have to wait its turn if you don't quit your bellyaching. How many times do I have to tell you that we can't let the woman catch sight of us?"

Belcher rolled his eyes but had the good sense not to argue. Behind him rode another man killer Quid had hired in Tucson, a pudgy leather slapper who went by the handle of Fergy, short for Ferguson.

Quid faced front. Half a mile ahead was the slender column of dust being raised by William Randolph's bunch. He slowed even more, unwilling to risk getting too close. The dull clank of a horseshoe on stone sounded to his right as Bob Plunkett came up alongside of him.

"Mind if we jaw a spell, pard?" the old scout asked.

"What's on your mind?"

Plunkett also marked the position of the dust. It tickled him to think that before too long they would do what the army, the law and every other bounty hunter in the territory had been unable to do for months on end: make wolf meat of the White Apache. Speaking low, so the new gunnies would not overhear, he said, "I want the truth, Ben. Are you really fixin' to share the bounty with that damned clotheshorse from New York City?"

Quid wasn't surprised by the question. No one knew him better than the scout. "What do you think?" he said.

"I reckon you'll play along with the jackass until Clay Taggart is lyin' dead at your feet. Then the dude is in for a big shock. Him and the woman, both."

"And they're not the only ones," Quid said, referring to the five men he had hired in Tucson. To his way of thinking, Belcher and Fergy, as well as the three riding with Randolph and Amelia Taggart, were expendable. He had brought them along in case the White Apache did not come to Devil's Canyon alone. Once they had served their purpose, he'd pay them off in lead.

Quid saw no earthly reason to cut them in for part of the bounty. After all he had gone through, he deserved a full half share. He was tempted to dispose of Plunkett, too, but the old man's tracking skills would come in mighty handy later on when they went after other outlaws.

The scout had an idea that brought a grin of anticipation to his lips. "If you want, I'll take care of the female. It's been a while since I carved one up. I can use the practice."

"Suit yourself," Quid said testily, his conscience pricked. Amelia Taggart was a decent woman. If there were some way to spare her, he would, but he had to face facts. She wasn't about to keep quiet. She'd go straight to the governor and tell how her cousin was lured into a trap, how the reporter and the others met their end. No, he couldn't let that happen. She had to die.

Bob Plunkett studied the landmarks ahead. "We'll be there before dark, I reckon."

The big bounty hunter nodded. "As I recollect, the trail to the top is on the north side."

"It is," the scout confirmed. He scratched his stubble, then sniffed his armpits. "A fella sure does get whiffy in this desert country, don't he? Keeps up, I might have to take my annual bath ten months early." He meant it as a joke.

For as long as Plunkett could remember, he had been taking one bath and one bath only each and every year. Everyone knew that too many were bad for a person's health. As his great-grandmother had warned him when he was knee-high to a calf, "Too much washin' makes a body sickly and weak. If the Good Lord had meant for us to spend all our time soakin' in water, he would've gave us gills."

Quid checked behind them. It never paid to grow careless in Apache country, and Devil's Canyon was right at the edge of the Chiricahua homeland.

"What do you aim to do with your share of the bounty?" Plunkett asked idly.

"I haven't given it much thought," Quid said. "Maybe go to Denver. I hear the doves there are as thick as fleas on an old coon dog."

"You can have your tainted whores," Plunkett said. "Me, I'm partial to young females as pure as driven snow." He smacked his lips. "That Taggart woman is a mite older than I like, but I can make do." Leaning toward Quid, he said softly, "Do you want to hear what I have in mind?"

"I'd rather not. I just had a piece of jerky, and I want it to stay in my stomach."

The scout thought that hilarious.

To the east, Amelia Taggart looked up as a gust of hot wind fanned her hair. "Did you hear that?" she asked.

William Randolph sat slumped in the saddle in front of her. The insufferable heat was taking its toll; his body felt as if he had spent most of the day baking in an oven. Licking his parched lips, he wiped a hand across his perspiring brow and turned. "Hear what, my dear?" he said, in keeping with his act of being her good friend.

"I don't know for sure," Amelia said. It had sounded like distant laughter, but it might just as well have been her ears playing tricks on her. The blazing sun befuddled her senses to the point where half the time she rode along in a dazed stupor.

"I heard nothing," Randolph assured her.

A dozen yards in front of them was Stirco. To their rear were Wilson and Carver. The gunmen were supposed to stay alert, but the inferno had taken its toll on them as well. Carver dozed. Wilson looked ready to collapse.

The reporter took a handkerchief from a pocket and wiped his face and neck. He would have given anything for a bucket of ice. Or, better yet, a dip in the Hudson. A nice, leisurely swim, late at night, just as he had done so many times as a boy. It had been ages since he last recalled those carefree days. The mere thought of being enveloped from head to toe in cold water was invigorating, but only for a few seconds. Imagination could not compete with reality.

Randolph started to lift the canteen that was dangling from his saddle horn by a leather strap. He didn't count on anyone noticing, but he was mistaken.

"I'd save that water if I were you, sir," Stirco said.

The reporter hesitated. He wanted a drink so badly, he could barely stand it. Without one, he feared he might keel over.

"Remember my orders," Stirco said. "I'm to make sure you get to Devil's Canyon with your hide intact. So far as we know, a spring is there. But if it's dried up since anyone last paid the place a visit, we'll need every drop of water we have to make it back out."

Amelia Taggart had been listening with half an ear. She was more interested in the stark mountains before them, so it took a few moments for the gunman's words to register. Perking up, she said, "His orders? What does he mean by that, Mr. Randolph? You're the one in charge."

Randolph mentally cursed Stirco for being so careless. "Of course I am," he replied suavely. "I was the one he referred to. He was simply reminding me of instructions I gave him before we left Tucson."

"Oh," Amelia said, not completely convinced. It had struck her as strange back in Tucson when Randolph had let her know that he was going to go find suitable men to take along, and not 15 minutes later he had been back, saying he had come across three who fit the bill quite by chance. Later, as they prepared to leave town, she could not help but notice the many smirks the trio bestowed upon her, as well as their constant whispering. It confirmed her ever growing suspicion that William Randolph was up to something. Amelia had tried telling herself that she was making the proverbial mountain out of a molehill, that there must be innocent explanations for everything the reporter had done, but she could deceive herself no longer. The nearer they drew to their destination, the more worried Amelia became because any plot Randolph was hatching had to involve Clay.

Amelia had thought that by obtaining a safe-conduct pass for her cousin, she could keep him from harm. Now, she was not so sure. There might be a way to get around it.

The big question Amelia had to answer was why. What did Randolph hope to gain? He had claimed that his sole interest in helping her was to write a series of articles for the *New York Sun*, and she had taken him at his word. But what if he had lied? What if he wasn't after a great story, as he put it. What if he were after the reward money?

Amelia looked at him, at his expensive hat and suit and his fancy shoes. Randolph had shown her that he liked to live well. He always wanted to stay at the best hotels, to eat at the best restaurants, to dress in the finest clothes money could buy. And money didn't grow on trees.

She should have seen it sooner, Amelia chided herself. In her eagerness to see Clay again, in her rush to help him, she let herself be blind to the dozens of little clues which should have alerted her that all was not as it seemed. Had she seen the truth sooner, she could have called the whole thing off.

Now it was too late to turn back. In a short while they would be at the site Randolph had picked.

For all she knew, Clay had already come across one of the 40 or 50 circulars they had posted on their long trek from Tucson. At that very moment he might be on his way to see her.

Astride a sorrel, Clay Taggart sped like the wind to the northeast, toward Devil's Canyon. He flew past manzanitas, past mesquite, past cactus, and hardly noticed them. He spooked deer, lizards and birds, but paid them no heed. In his mind all he could see was the circular Delgadito had found:

CLAY TAGGART
OTHERWISE KNOWN AS THE WHITE APACHE. YOUR COUSIN AMELIA WANTS YOU TO MEET HER AT DEVIL'S CANYON WITHIN 30 DAYS OF THE DATE ON THIS CIRCULAR. SEE THE LIGHT OF REASON. END THE BLOODSHED. DO WHAT IS RIGHT AND HEAR HER OUT. WHAT HAVE YOU GOT TO LOSE?

Clay posed the query aloud as he skirted a saguaro. "What have I got to lose?" The answer was as plain as the nose on his face: his life. On first reading the message, he had been partial to the notion that the invite had been concocted to draw him into an ambush. But the more he had thought about it, the more he decided that it couldn't be.

No one in Arizona, absolutely no one at all, knew about his cousin. He had never mentioned her to a living soul, never even talked about his childhood.

Why should he? It was painful for him to dwell on their wonderful friendship. Those had been some of the happiest years of his life, and recollecting them sparked anew the gut-wrenching hurt he had felt the day they parted company. For weeks afterward Clay had held a grudge against his pa.

In time, however, the hurt had faded. To keep it from cropping up again, he had shut Amelia from his mind.

Now she was back, and Clay was at a loss to know what to do. Seeing her was the first step, but then what? Why was she there? What did she hope to accomplish? The circular had said to "see the light of reason," to "end the bloodshed." What the hell did that mean? he mused. Was she going to try and convince him to turn himself in?

There were so many questions and so few answers.

Rather than wear himself out trying to solve the mystery, Clay buckled down to the task of covering as much ground as he could before sunset. By pushing hard, but not hard enough to ride the sorrel into the ground, he stood to reach the rendezvous site in three days. Each one would be an eternity of suspense.

Clay found himself reliving his childhood, recalling the joyful times he'd shared with Amelia, dredging up memories long forgotten.

It was a grave lapse in judgment. A man wanted by every lawdog in the territory, a man every Arizonan would like to see come down with hemp fever and do a strangulation jig, could not afford to let his guard down. Yet that is exactly what Clay Taggart did. He trotted on across the broad expanse of chaparral, so deep in thought that he was unaware others were nearby until a rifle retort rang out and the whine of lead off a rock made him snap around.

A bunch of cowboys swept toward him, several tugging long guns from saddle scabbards. A lanky scarecrow already had his out. Clay counted, seven, eight, nine, then another shot came closer than the first and he poked his heels into the sorrel and lit a shuck. Yips and hollers mixed with more shots, none of which scored.

Clay called himself an idiot and a lot of other names besides. Lead flew fast and furious around him, growing closer as the hands got the range. He did not return fire. To hit anything from horseback he had to slow down, and the moment he did, the punchers would pick him off.

He tried to recollect if a remote ranch was in the vicinity. It was so far out in the sticks that the hillbilly brush hands thirsting for his blood were probably lucky to strike town once a month. The men who worked for such outfits were always fiercely loyal to the brand. To them, he was an Apache, an enemy, a threat to their employer and his cattle. They'd chase him clear to Canada, if need be. He had to shake them, and quickly, before one made a lucky shot or the sorrel played out.

To the northwest beckoned a wall of mesquite, bristling with thorns. No ranny worthy of the name would take a horse in there. Clay counted on that as he reined to the left and lowered his chest to the sorrel's broad back.

Nine guns were booming in a thunderous din. Some of the shots came much too close for comfort. One nicked the sorrel's shoulder. Clay twisted and fired twice, wasting ammo in the hope of forcing the cowboys to fall back, but he might as well have used a slingshot. Those punchers did not wear all that hardware for bluff or ballast. They were not about to quit.

Clay sought an opening in the thorn wall. There had to be one, but none was evident. Cutting to the right, he paralleled the mesquite, the sorrel raising enough dust to make it hard for the cowboys to get a clear shot. They were fanning out, paralleling *him* to prevent him from doubling back on them or outdistancing them. Each was a seasoned cowman. They knew how to herd any critter alive, including the two-legged variety, into a tight corner, how to box in their quarry so that escape was impossible.

The sorrel ran superbly but it wasn't the black stallion. Clay could see that already two of the cowboys had looped around ahead of him and were angling to cut him off. Once that happened it was all over. He might blast his way past them, but they would delay him long enough for the rest to surround him and turn his body into a sieve.

Then a gap appeared in the mesquite. Not knowing if it was a trail or a blind alley, Clay swerved the sorrel into it. On either side the branches were so close that the thorns would rip his legs to shreds if he did not clamp them tightly to his mount. He had to straighten to see where he was going, and in doing so exposed his head and shoulders to his pursuers. A gunpowder litany rocked the chaparral. Something snatched at his hat but it stayed on.

The gap widened slightly. It angled to the north. Clay made the turn, discovered a godsend in the form of a long, straight stretch and whipped the reins against the sorrel's neck.

Clay had hoped that the cowboys would not plunge into the maze of thorns, but a glance back revealed that they wanted him so badly that four of them were willing to risk life and limb, as well as the welfare of their mounts, to catch him. Four had followed him in. The rest were spreading to the right and left, seeking a way around so they could cut him off before he found a way out.

Clay might have outsmarted himself. Unless he gained open ground before the punchers headed him off, he would be trapped. It would only be a matter of time before they put windows in his skull.

A few of the cowhands still fired every so often but most were waiting for clear shots.

Clay came to another bend. At a trot he rushed around it—and saw a wall of mesquite blocking his path. He hauled hard on the reins, bringing the sorrel to a sliding stop. In a spray of dust they halted mere inches from the barrier. He was trapped! The only way to go was back the way he had come.

Or was it?

To Clay's left was a narrow opening. Quickly dismounting, holding the reins, he stepped closer. It was a path leading deeper into the labyrinth, but it was barely wide enough for the sorrel. If it narrowed farther in, he would be as good as dead. Since he had no choice, he took it.

On foot, leading the sorrel, Clay threaded a serpentine course into the heart of the mesquite. Very soon he lost track of exactly where he was in relation to the point where he had entered. He had no idea whether he could find his way out again.

The only advantage was that now the mesquite was high enough to hide them. He paused to listen, to pinpoint the positions of his enemies, just as a gruff voice rang out.

"Where the hell did he go? I can't see him!"

"Me neither, Charley."

"Just keep lookin', boys. That red bastard is in here somewhere, and we're agoin' to blow out his lamp!"

Clay went on. Yet another turn loomed ahead.

Desert Fury

He took it slowly, half afraid the trail would end at another thorn wall. It did peter out, all right, but at a small circular area bare of growth, a clearing eight feet in diameter. A brainstorm came to him.

Guiding the sorrel to the middle, White Apache stooped, bent one of its front legs back as far as it would go, then gripped the bridle and let his body go slack so that the animal's neck bore most of his weight. The sorrel resisted, but only for a few moments. Giving in to the inevitable, the horse slowly sank down, and he let go of its leg. Taking a seat beside it, he stroked the animal's neck.

Now all he could do was bide his time.

The cowboys were a persistent bunch. For hours they roved the mesquite, those on the outside circling around and around, those on the inside searching every twisting trail. They yelled back and forth a lot. As time dragged on, their confidence was replaced by baffled anger.

The sun was low in the sky when the man remarked for all to hear, "We should have found the mangy son of a bitch by now! I say we mosey on before it gets dark."

"We keep looking," someone responded curtly.

"Be reasonable, Baker," the first man said. "The big sugar is expectin' us back by nightfall. If we ain't there, he'll throw a fit. And I'd rather be stomped by an ornery bull than face our boss when his dander is up."

"He'll understand, Grimes," Baker said. "Apaches killed his wife, remember? We're under standing orders to kill every one of the vermin we see."

"Well, we won't be killin' this one," Grimes insisted. "Don't ask me how, but he's done givin' us the slip."

"That's an Apache for you," said a third man.

133

"They're as slippery as a passel of eels."

The hunt went on, but not for much longer. Baker finally called out, "Enough is enough, boys. I reckon Grimes has a point. We're wasting our time. Let's light a shuck for the ranch."

Clay Taggart sighed gratefully. He thought he would soon be on his way again, until a cowhand hollered.

"Baker! I can't find the trail that brought me in here! How the dickens am I supposed to get out?"

"What do you use for brains, Haverman?" Baker answered. "Didn't you keep track of where you were going?"

"Not exactly."

Several of the cowboys laughed. Baker swore, then said, "Backtrack yourself, then. That shouldn't be too hard."

"I can't. I got so twisted around, it wouldn't do me any good."

Someone chortled. "Leave it to Haverman! That boy don't have the brains God gave a yucca!"

"Can anyone see him?" Baker shouted.

Apparently no one could. Haverman was too far in. Clay Taggart heard the man, though, moving slowly toward him. The dull clump of hooves grew louder. Suddenly the puncher yelled excitedly.

"Baker! The rest of you! I found some tracks, but I don't think they're mine. They must belong to the Apache!"

"Damn!" Baker replied. "Take it slow, boy! If he's still in there, he knows right where you are."

"I ain't scared of no red heathen."

White Apache clenched his rifle. He had no desire to kill the young cowhand. He would rather the man turned back and left him alone. Then hooves drummed, and a lanky figure materialized on top of a bay. Haverman rushed around the last bend, spotted him and raised a pistol. White Apache fired just once.

For a few moments, silence greeted the blast. Baker called Haverman's name. Others joined in. When the cowboy did not answer, curses turned the air blue. Finally Baker quieted them and said, "The stinking Apache got him! But he's not going to get away with it! Grimes! Dixon! Pedro! Fan out! We're going to flush the scum out!"

"How?" a puncher asked.

"How else? We'll set this patch of mesquite on fire!"

Chapter Ten

Another day was drawing to a close. Deep in the winding recesses of Devil's Canyon, the shadows lengthened quickly once the sun dipped below the rim of the towering rock walls.

Amelia Taggart did not like it there. She tried telling herself that it was because the narrow canyon gave her a constant feeling of being hemmed in. But she was so inherently honest that she could not deceive herself for long. The real reason had nothing to do with the canyon and everything to do with one of the gunmen.

The hawkish gunman called Stirco had been eyeing her on the sly. Amelia had not noticed it until a few hours ago. By sheer chance she had happened to glance out of the corner of her eye and noticed the man giving her the sort of hungry look men normally reserved for fallen doves out strutting their physical wares. It had angered her but she had not made an issue of his rude behavior. She felt confident he would not try anything, not with Randolph and the other men there.

Then it occurred to Amelia that the other gunmen were Stirco's friends. And William Randolph did not impress her as being able to fend off a riled rabbit, let alone a frontier tough. Whether Randolph was morally stalwart enough even to try to defend a lady's honor was debatable. If Stirco tried to take liberties, she might need to fend for herself. Isolated as they were, outnumbered as she was, the outcome was a foregone conclusion.

Amelia shut the worry from her mind. As her pa had always liked to say, she would cross that bridge when she came to it. In the meantime, she had Clay to think of. Now that they had reached the rendezvous site, the prospect of seeing him again was imminent. She needed to work out ahead of time what she was going to say. She had to find the right words to persuade him to forsake the blood-stained path he had chosen and to give himself up.

Devil's Canyon ended at a high cliff. Massive boulders dotted its base and lined the bottom of the south wall. Among them, hidden from view until a person was right on it, was a clear, cold spring. Fully 10 feet across, it formed a waist-high pool.

They had only been there an hour or so. All of them had drunk their full, and the horses had been watered. Amelia sat on a small boulder, her hands folded in her lap, and scanned the ramparts on both sides. Preoccupied with thoughts of Clay, she did not hear the reporter come up.

"What are you looking at?" William Randolph demanded. Now that his plan had reached the critical point, he was growing more and more nervous. It bothered him to see her studying the heights. Quid and Plunkett were up there lying in wait. They were supposed to be near the canyon entrance, well out of sight, but Randolph would not risk her accidentally spotting them.

"Nothing much," Amelia said, puzzled by his strained tone and anxious manner.

"Oh, I thought you might have seen something," Randolph said and promptly regretted being so stupid. It would not do to have her suspect that he was in league with the men who would soon slay her cousin.

Amelia jumped to the obvious conclusion. "Are you worried about the renegades?"

They were the last thing on Randolph's mind, but he nodded and said, "Who wouldn't be?" Not caring to sound like a coward, he added, "Not for my own sake, you understand, but for yours. I've heard stories. Apache do terrible things to their captives. Why, even if they let you live, you'd be forced to take up with a buck."

"I'd kill myself before I would let any man violate me," Amelia declared loud enough for Stirco and the others to hear.

"I hope it won't come to that," Randolph said, and he was sincere. He had never meant for the woman to come to any harm. Walking off, he stared back down the dark canyon. How soon would it be, he wondered, before Clay Taggart showed up? He scoured the sheer sides, hoping Benjamin Quid was right about there only being one way in. If not, the consequences were too horrible to contemplate.

Amelia watched the reporter, seeking clues to confirm her suspicion that he was up to something. The feeling of someone watching her caused her to shift. She caught Stirco in the act of brazenly ogling her figure. To show her annoyance, she glared. To her dismay, he smiled, as if being a lecher were a joke, and casually turned back to the task of getting their fire started.

Amelia almost marched over to confront him. She would not tolerate being treated as if she were a common prostitute. Some women might enjoy it, but she wasn't one of them. Her folks had raised her to take pride in herself, and never to let anyone besmirch her dignity.

For the moment, Amelia did nothing. As the Good Book put it, there was a time and a place for everything, and Amelia judged it to be the wrong time to turn Stirco and his companions openly against her. Not when Clay might arrive at any time. They had been told about the safe-conduct pass so they would not take it into their heads to shoot him on sight. But she would not put it past them to do so anyway, especially if they held a grudge against her.

Amelia placed a hand on the small handbag she had toted from St. Louis. In it were her few cosmetics, for she was not one of those women who lavished powder and rouge and such on her face. Also in it was something that had belonged to her pa, something she had not parted with once since the long journey began, something no one else knew she carried, not even Randolph. It was an old, single-shot pocket pistol manufactured by Henry Derringer. A .41 caliber, it happened to be the exact same model used by John Wilkes Booth to assassinate Pres. Abraham Lincoln.

It reassured Amelia to know she could defend herself if attacked. Stirco and his ilk were bigger and stronger than she was, but any advantage their size gave them was more than offset by the gun. Few bad men would tempt fate by going up against a loaded revolver in the hands of someone determined to use it. That was one of the reason the framers of the Constitution included the right to bear arms as the Second Amendment.

Amelia did not see anything wrong with guns. They were tools, nothing more. Tools she had been around all her life. Her father and brother had used rifles regularly to hunt game. Her brother had been fond of a nickel-plated Remington he took with him when he signed on to fight for the Union cause. Many times she had taken a rifle and gone into the woods after game for the supper pot. So she had no qualms about using the pistol in her bag. Let Stirco or anyone else try something, and she would blow a hole in them the size of her fist.

William Randolph saw the woman smile and assumed she was thinking about her impending reunion with her cousin. It made him smile. She was so gullible, it was pathetic. Soon Clay Taggart would be dead, and all her good intentions would never bring him back to life again.

It had been preordained, William told himself, from the moment he put the White Apache at the top of his list. He had manipulated her from the beginning, and he would go on doing so after her cousin was dead.

In that great, complex chess game of life, William Randolph flattered himself that he had no equals. As Miss Amelia Taggart would shortly find out the hard way.

The instant the young cowhand named Haverman toppled from the saddle, White Apache leaped and caught hold of the bay's bridle before it could run off. Holding fast, he spoke softly to the horse to calm it, while stroking its neck.

White Apache heard the cowboys shout back

and forth. He heard the foreman, Baker, say that they were going to set the mesquite ablaze.

"Are you loco?" one of the others demanded. "We do that, we're liable to burn half the country-side."

"Like hell," Baker insisted. "This here stand is sitting all by its lonesome in the middle of no-where. We can burn it down without having to worry about setting fire to anything else."

"It doesn't seem safe to me," said someone else.

Baker was not about to budge. "We're not let-ting the savage get away, and that's final. We owe Haverman at least that much. Now do as I tell you without kicking like a bay steer."

White Apache heard the thud of hooves on all sides. Rising onto his toes, he saw riders to the north, south, east and west. It gave him some no-tion of how large an area the mesquite covered, about four or five acres. He hunkered before any of the hands spotted him.

Then, for the longest, nerve-racking while, all was quiet. The sun, a blazing skillet, rested on the rim of the earth. It began to sink lower although not fast enough to suit White Apache. He wanted to make his bid for escape under the cover of en-croaching darkness.

Suddenly the sorrel raised its head and sniffed loudly. A few seconds later the bay did the same, then nickered. White Apache tilted his head back, inhaled, and smelled the unmistakable acrid scent of smoke. The mesquite had been set ablaze.

Since the wind was blowing from the north-west, White Apache figured the flames would eat toward him from that direction.

On the bay was Haverman's lariat. Helping him-self to it, Clay Taggart slid the loop over the bay's neck. With the rope in one hand, and the sorrel's reins as well as the Winchester in the other, he started to retrace his steps, bearing to the south at every junction. It was slow going since he had to keep low. Every now and then he rose high enough to scan the mesquite, and it was one of those times that he spied flames to the north. A little farther on, Clay looked again. Now there were flames to the east and west, as well.

The cowboys had set the mesquite on fire at all four points of the compass. The flames were rapidly converging, and once they linked up, he would be completely encircled.

White Apache could no longer afford the luxury of caution. Climbing onto the sorrel, he went faster, sticking to a southerly bearing. Soon he realized that the wind had shifted, as it often did at that time of the day. Now it pushed the flames from the southwest and they were advancing at an alarming rate, devouring the mesquite as a starved man might devour a plate of prime beef.

The smoke grew thicker. It swirled above the stand, settling when the wind briefly died now and again, hugging the top of the growth like a gray blanket. A roiling cloud of it swept toward White Apache. He held his breath just in time. In moments he was shrouded from head to toe in a swirling fog that stung his eyes and filled his nostrils even though he wasn't breathing. The horses snorted and pranced.

White Apache could not see the trail ahead, and had to slow to a crawl. He swatted at the smoke before his eyes but it did no good.

For over two minutes White Apache blundered on. Cupping a hand over his mouth, he took short breaths. He failed to pay attention to where he was going and unknowingly veered to the left. Thorns bit into his leg so he veered to the right, to where he thought the middle of the trail should be. In all the smoke, he misjudged and more thorns pricked his right leg.

The sorrel whinnied, its side pierced by a score of razor-thin barbs.

"Hey, did you hear that?" a cowboy called.

"I sure did!" answered another. "Keep your eyes peeled, boys! It won't be long before he makes a break for it!"

Clay would have liked to, but he was more lost than ever. He couldn't see his hand at arm's length, let alone the way out. Unwilling to give up, he nudged the sorrel. Behind him, the bay balked, and he had to tug on the rope to keep the animal going.

It seemed to him that the smoke was growing thicker. Presently the crackle of flames and flashes of orange and red alerted him to a burning column of mesquite directly in front of him.

White Apache looked to the right and the left. Any side trails he might take were obscured by the smoke. He had to find one, and quickly, or he would be roasted alive.

There wasn't enough room to turn around, so, slipping from the saddle, White Apache led the horses forward, a halting step at a time. Flames flared to his left. More blossomed to his right. The heat blistered him worse than the desert sun at midday. The air grew stifling, so much so that his lungs ached for a fresh breath.

A wave of intense heat stopped White Apache dead. Weakness claimed him. His knees buckled. He caught himself before he fell, clung to the sorrel, and was about to attempt to swing the animal around when he glimpsed what seemed to be an opening almost at his right elbow. He was unable to tell if it was another trail. Desperate, he stepped into the gap, shielding his face with his forearm. Crackling fingers of hissing fire had engulfed the brush all around him.

White Apache shuffled forward. There was a trail, sure enough, a narrow one that twisted and turned every which way. Whether it would take him away from the fire or deeper into it, he couldn't say. Since it was the only trail he was likely to find, he had to take it.

Both horses shied, almost yanking White Apache off his feet. Holding tight, he dug in his heels and advanced. The trail narrowed. Thorns hemmed him in so close that he could not extend an arm to either side. He dreaded that he had reached the end of his rope, that the trail would end and he would be trapped by the flames.

To the east a cowboy shouted. To the north someone responded. White Apache could not hear the words above the roar of the fire. Bending at the waist, he rounded a corner. A blast of flame gusted across the path. He threw himself backward but was too slow to avoid suffering a singed arm. Forgetting himself in his pain, he inhaled.

Searing agony lanced through White Apache's chest. Staggering, he erupted in a coughing fit which would not end. Every breath he took only made it worse, thanks to the soup-thick smoke. Falling to his knees, he doubled over, and by chance discovered a thin amount of untainted air close to the ground. He breathed greedily. When his lungs stopped hurting and his eyes stopped watering, he hurried on.

Flames writhed everywhere, transforming the chaparral into a living hell. White Apache had to fight the horses for every step he took. They were close to panic, the bay in particular.

"I can't see a damn thing!" one of the cowboys bellowed.

Neither could Clay. He bumped into a flaming limb, backpedaled, and went around another bend. The smoke thinned slightly. He thought that he saw an opening and broke into a brisk jog. In several strides he was in a large clearing, where he paused to take stock of the situation.

From out of the smoke solidified a figure on horseback. It was a puncher, and it was hard to say which of them was more surprised. The cowboy cursed and clawed for a pistol. White Apache snapped up the Winchester, his finger curling on the trigger. The barrel spat lead, which slammed into the man's sternum, ripped him from his horse and flung him into the gray veil.

White Apache was dumfounded that one of the punchers had ventured into the burning mesquite after him. The man had to have been loco, he mused. Then a powerful gust of wind parted the smoke, and where White Apache had expected to see more mesquite, he saw open prairie. It took a few moments for the reality to set in. He was out of the maze! He was in the clear! Now all he had to do was mount up and get the hell out of there.

But it wasn't quite that simple. To the right a cowboy hollered, "What were those shots about? Decker, was that you?"

Hooves thudded, coming closer. White Apache gripped the sorrel's mane and swung up.

"Decker? Where are you?"

To avoid another clash, Clay reined to the left and made off through the smoke at a walk so as not to make too much noise. His hopes were dashed when a pair of cowboys abruptly appeared in front of him. They were scanning the mesquite. One held a carbine, the other had a hand resting on the butt of a Colt. Both saw him at the same instant and went to bring their guns into play.

White Apache was already in motion. A jab of his heels sparked the sorrel into a gallop. He raced between the pair, the sorrel slamming into their mounts and barreling past. As he swept by, White Apache clubbed the puncher on the right with his Winchester while, at the same time, kicking out with his left leg and knocking the other man from the saddle.

A cloud of smoke sheathed White Apache as shots rang out. Lead buzzed on both sides. He did not return fire. Escaping was more important than slaying the punchers.

Fiero would not have thought so. For that matter, all the Chiricahua would have used the cover provided by the smoke to kill as many white-eyes as they could. It gave Clay Taggart a fleeting moment of doubt. How could he claim to be one of the renegades when, unlike them, he was willing to let their sworn enemies live?

The sound of pursuit derailed Clay's train of thought. Slanting to the right, he burst from the smoke into fresh air. The sun had set. Twilight claimed the landscape. He cut to the northeast, his original bearing, and rode full out, looking back every few seconds to see if any of the cowhands had spotted him.

They had. A lean brush hand trotted into view, yipped and gave chase. Seconds later another joined the first. They covered about 50 yards when a second pair showed up. The quartet applied their spurs with gusto.

Still holding the lead rope, White Apache went faster. A few shots zinged his way, but for the most part the cowboys concentrated on overtaking him.

They were superb horsemen, mounted on animals as fine as any anywhere. They could ride rings around most men. Their confidence showed in the set of their features and their whoops of excitement. They believed the outcome was inevitable.

But they did not know that the man they were after was not a full-blooded Apache. They had no idea that their quarry had once been a cowboy, just like them. That he had worked a ranch from dawn until well past dusk, day in and day out, year after year, doing most of the work from horseback. He was one of them, or had been, a kindred spirit in a very real sense. But to the riding skills and savvy he had learned as a rancher had been added the exceptional abilities of his Chiricahua mentors.

So after a mile, the cowboys were no closer than they had been when they first gave chase. They looked at one another but did not quit. It went against their grain. Besides, their quarry was leading a second horse, and that was bound to slow the first one down, eventually.

Clay Taggart knew that, too. Which was why he monitored the sorrel closely, and when it showed signs of being winded, when it started to flag, he would be ready to make his move.

Clay had brought the bay along for a reason. It was his ace in the hole. He slowed just a little and began to coil the rope, pulling the bay toward him. Soon it was galloping at his side.

For half a mile more Clay sped along through the gathering darkness. When next he checked over his shoulder, the four cowboys were vague shapes at the limit of his vision. Their mounts, like the sorrel, would be growing tired. It was time to play his trump card.

Clay tugged on the rope to draw the bay a little

closer still. Every inch counted. Switching the Winchester from his right hand to his left, he coiled his legs up under him so that he balanced on the sorrel's back on his heels. Tensing, he pushed off and leaped to the right, sailing in a tight arc that brought him down squarely atop the bay. He flung his legs wide to fork leather.

All should have gone well. Clay had timed his jump perfectly. But at the very instant he sprang, the horses came to a knoll and flew up the steep slope. It put the bay's back at a sharp angle. Instead of alighting in the center of the saddle, as Clay had counted on, he came down on the cantle. Pain speared his groin and shot up his spine. He began to slip to the left. Lunging, he grabbed at the saddle horn, but he missed it because the horse had hit a rut and stumbled. It threw him backward, over the cowboy's bedroll. For several harrowing heartbeats he swayed, about to pitch off the animal's rump. His flailing fingers found the cantle. He held on for dear life.

The bay righted itself. Clay was thrown forward. This time he caught hold of the horn and was not about to let go. Exerting every muscle in his right arm, he hauled himself up and over the bedroll and the cantle. At last his legs draped over the saddle. His feet found the stirrups and slipped into them. Leaning down, he snagged the dangling reins.

It felt strange to have a saddle under him again, after so many months of riding bareback. It brought back memories Clay would rather not dwell on. Gaining the top of the knoll, he looked back. The cowboys were closer, but they were in for a big surprise.

The sorrel, now riderless, was beginning to slow. Clay swatted it with the Winchester and it angled to the north at a trot. Perhaps it would lure the cowboys off. If not, Clay wasn't worried. The bay was fresher than their horses. It would rapidly outdistance them.

True to his prediction, five minutes later there was no sign of his pursuers. Clay Taggart, the White Apache, streaked across the vast Arizona wilderness under a myriad of sparkling stars, a brisk north wind fanning his face, fondness for his cousin fanning the flames of his heart. He was hell-bent for leather to reach Devil's Canyon as soon as possible. He couldn't wait to see Amelia again. But if she wasn't there, if it was a trap, those responsible were going to pay—in blood.

Chapter Eleven

Morning dawned crisp and clear. Benjamin Quid, perched on the north rim of Devil's Canyon, where he could see the canyon mouth and the approaches to it, shifted position to relieve a cramp in his calf. He had been standing watch since three in the morning, and he was tired.

Quid leaned against a boulder and took the makings for a cigarette from his shirt pocket. Once he had it lit, he puffed slowly, savoring the taste. He was not concerned about the smoke giving his position away. In the first place, he doubted that Clay Taggart would show up for days. In the second, he was so high up, Taggart would need to have the eyes of an eagle to spot the few wispy tendrils that rose above the boulder.

Quid was not going to make the mistake so many did and make Taggart out to be more than the man was. Because of the many tall tales about the White Apache's bloody exploits, folks had taken to regarding Taggart as some sort of human demon. Some claimed he was a ghost who could appear and disappear at will. A few asserted that he was damned near invincible, that Apache magic had rendered him bullet proof.

It was all nonsense, of course. Taggart was clever and had more lives than a cat, but he had no superhuman powers. The only reason the turncoat had gotten the better of Quid the first time they tangled was due to Plunkett's carelessness. The old scout had assured Quid that there had not been another living soul within miles of the spring. Since Plunkett had never been wrong before, Quid had accepted his word and let down his guard.

Never again. Quid had learned his lesson. Or, rather, *relearned* it. Early on in the bounty business he had found that a manhunter had to be cat eyed all the time or he wouldn't last long. Especially if, like Quid, the bounty hunter only went after those who had the highest bounties on their heads—usually, hard cases wanted for murder or other violent crimes, men who would kill anyone who tried to take them in.

Quid had claimed over 20 bounties. Never once had any of the men he sought beaten him at his own game—until Clay Taggart, that is.

Quid tingled at the thought of having the bastard lined up in his rifle sights. Only taking the body back to Tucson for one and all to see would erase the shame of their first encounter. In the bargain he might earn some spare change by charging admission, as was often done with notorious outlaws. Plenty of people would be willing to part with two bits for the privilege of boasting that they had seen the White Apache's corpse. Quid might even sell snips of Taggart's hair and offer them for 50 cents each.

"Is that smoke worth your life, Ben?"

Quid had not heard Plunkett come up on him, and started. "Damn," he growled, embarrassed that he had been taken unawares. "Don't sneak up on a man like that or you're liable to eat lead."

Plunkett moved to the edge to survey the canyon. "You've never fought Apache like I have, or you'd know they're two-legged bloodhounds. A buck could smell that cigarette of yours from a mile off."

"Spare me another tall tale," Quid said. Defiantly, he took a long drag and blew a small cloud into the air.

The scout glanced at his partner. It was rare for the big man to speak so harshly to him. "What's gotten into your craw?"

"Nothing," Quid lied.

Plunkett was too shrewd to be fooled. "Seems to me that you're lettin' this White Apache get under your skin. So what if he licked us once? This time we have an edge." Hunkering, he plucked the dry stem of a withered plant and stuck it between his front teeth. "It ain't like you to get all flustered. Keep it up and you'll worry me."

"I'm not flustered!" Quid snapped. "It's just that I want him dead so badly, I can damned near taste it."

"Which is just as bad, I reckon," Plunkett said. "Revenge makes a man reckless. A person in our line of work has to keep their wits about 'em at all times. So don't let Taggart drive you to the wall."

Quid did not like being lectured. "Don't worry about me, old man. When the time comes, I'll be ready." To avoid any more talk on the subject, he stalked off, along the rim. It was 75 yards from the spot they had selected for the ambush to the first bend in the canyon. Over a quarter of a mile past the bend lay the spring where Taggart's cousin waited.

Nothing moved down there. Yet. Quid walked to where the pudgy gunman, Fergy, knelt in a wide cleft. In his current frame of mind, if he had caught Fergy sleeping, there would have been hell to pay. But the gunman was awake, fiddling with a spur.

Looking up, Fergy said, "Anything wrong, boss?"

"No." Quid paused to gaze out over the foothills that led up to the canyon, and the plain beyond. "Bob just relieved me. I'll send Belcher up to spell you in a few minutes."

Fergy grinned. "It won't be long until Taggart shows, will it? I can't wait to get my hands on my share. It's more money than I've ever had at one time in my whole life."

Quid stared at the unsuspecting gunny. Little did Fergy realize that Belcher and he would never spend a cent of the reward. He turned to go.

"I've been meaning to ask you a favor," Fergy said.

The big man faced him.

"You're a fair hombre to work for. If you ever need an extra gun again, I hope you'll keep me in mind."

"I can always use a good man. Survive this," Quid said soberly, "and we'll see."

"Don't you worry. The White Apache isn't about to blow out my lamp if I can help it."

Nodding, Quid headed for their camp. A prick of conscience troubled him but he shrugged it off. He couldn't let feelings get in his way, not where money was concerned. That wouldn't be professional.

* * *

Amelia Taggart awoke with a start. For a while she lay staring at the top of her tent and wondering what had awakened her so rudely. She did not recall having a nightmare. Then, as she was about to close her eyes and snatch a little more sleep, her intuition flared. She experienced the most peculiar feeling that someone was watching her.

Rolling toward the front, Amelia was shocked to see the flap fluttering, as if it had just been closed. Yet that couldn't be. She had tied it shut prior to retiring.

Rising to her knees, a blanket held tightly around her shoulders, Amelia scooted over. She gripped the edge and pulled. To her horror, the flap swung freely. The tie string was on the ground.

At a loss to understand how her bow knot had come undone, Amelia examined the tie. Her consternation grew when she discovered the cord had been cut. Someone had slipped a hand under the bottom of the flap and silently sliced it while she slept.

Amelia parted the flap enough to see the camp. There was no sign of Randolph, but the three gunmen were up and about. Wilson was toting water from the spring. Carver tended the horses. Nearest the tent, preparing coffee at the fire, was Stirco. The man glanced at the tent, saw her and smirked.

What gall! Amelia thought to herself. Infuriated, she closed the flap and swiftly donned her everyday dress, as she called it. Clutching her handbag, she stepped out into the bright morning sunshine.

The canyon was deathly still, unlike her farm where birds would be chirping, chickens clucking, and sheep bleating. How she missed it!

At that moment, William Randolph emerged

from his tent, yawning and scratching his chin. In his opinion it was an ungodly hour to be getting up. But he was so excited by the possibility of Clay Taggart soon appearing that he had not slept well at all. The early morning commotion outside his tent had not helped in that regard.

Frontier types, Randolph had learned, invariably rose with the sun, or before, and for the life of him, he could not comprehend how they did it. His best guess was that they did not need as much sleep as he did because their doltish minds did not use as much energy during the day.

Randolph noticed the woman. He forced a smile. "Good morning, Miss Taggart. You're up earlier than usual, aren't you?"

Amelia did not reply. She had eyes only for Stirco. Marching up to him, she slipped a hand into her bag and palmed the pocket pistol. Boldly, she declared, "If you ever do that again, you will be sorry."

The gunman acted surprised. "What are you talking about, ma'am? All I'm doing is fixing coffee."

"You know very well what I am referring to," Amelia said, her anger fueled by his denial. "I am a lady, not a fallen dove. You will accord me the respect I deserve or suffer accordingly."

William Randolph had never heard the woman speak so harshly to anyone. "What's going on?" he asked. "What is this all about?"

"Ask the lecher," Amelia said. Pivoting on a heel, she walked to the spring to wash up. Wilson doffed his hat to her, so she acknowledged the greeting with a nod. Moving around to the far side of the pool, she sat and dipped her hand in the cool water.

Inwardly, Amelia seethed. It was the old Taggart temper, the one great weakness of the Taggart clan. Her pa had it; her brother had it; and she had it. So too, she figured, did her cousin Clay.

The Taggarts had always been slow to come to a boil, but once they did, they were capable of exploding in the most savage violence. She could still recall the time a drunk made an improper remark to her mother. Her father had beaten the scoundrel within an inch of his life.

Splashing her face and neck, Amelia fought to calm herself. By letting Stirco rile her, she was lowering herself to his crude level. She could only pray that her warning had served its purpose. If not, the man would rue the day they met.

Amelia gazed wistfully up the canyon, wondering where her cousin might be, and if he were aware of the circulars yet. She imagined him flying to her side, as anxious to see her again as she was to see him.

Clay Taggart had ridden all night long. He had pushed the bay mercilessly, something he would never have done during his years of ranching. Now, the day less than an hour old, he had about ridden the animal into the ground. It was caked with lather, wheezing like a stricken ox. He knew that he should stop, that it dearly needed rest, but he did not slacken his pace.

An internal urge spurred Clay on, an impulse to reach his cousin swiftly. He could not say what caused it. Maybe it was the bond they once shared. Maybe it was the fact that his cousin cared enough to go to all this trouble to see him. Maybe it was simply their being kin.

Kin. The word echoed in the caverns of Clay's mind, reminding him that the Taggart clan had always been tight knit, until the day his pa up and herded his family westward. He sometimes gave thought to how much different his life would have been had his pa stayed back East.

It was strange, Clay reflected, how life worked out. A man never really knew from one minute to the next what fate had in store for him. It might be glory. It might be ruin. Or it might be an average life with few peaks and valleys. His main wish was that his life would end in a blaze of gunfire and not in a pathetic whimper.

A sudden lurch by the bay brought Clay back to the present. The bay was staggering on its last legs. Clay reined up and dismounted. Nickering, the horse shook itself, tried to go on, but faltered. Slowly, frothing at the mouth, it oozed to the ground.

White Apache cocked the Winchester, then pressed the muzzle to the animal's head. The bay was of no further use to him. A true Apache would shoot it and be done with it. His finger tightened on the trigger, but not enough for the hammer to strike the cartridge.

The bay looked at him, eyes wide in fright, as if sensing impending doom.

It was Clay Taggart, not the White Apache, who lowered the .44-40. It was Clay Taggart, not the White Apache, who stripped off the saddle and blanket. And it was Clay Taggart, not the White Apache, who gave the horse a quick rubdown before turning and jogging to the northeast.

But once the bay was out of sight, it was the White Apache, not Clay Taggart, who ate up the miles at a pace few white men could match. It was the White Apache, not Clay Taggart, whose whipcord frame was unaffected by the blazing sun. It was the White Apache, not Clay Taggart, who took a two-hour nap shortly before sunset, then resumed his trek as refreshed as if he had slept the whole night through.

Thanks to his Chiricahua friends, *Lickoyee-shisinday* knew many of the shortcuts only the Indians knew. So it was that he came within sight of the mouth of Devil's Canyon at approximately four o'clock the next morning.

Clay was so eager to see Amelia that he almost entered the canyon without first making sure he was not walking into a trap. Well shy of the entrance, he halted in the shadow of a rock slab. He had only been in the canyon once before, when the band had stopped at the spring on their way back to the Dragoons after a raid into Mexico. It was, as he recollected, long and narrow, ideal for a bushwhacking.

White Apache studied the canyon floor, the sheer walls, the remote, jagged heights. For over an hour he scrutinized every nook and cranny. When he had satisfied himself that no enemies were lying in wait, he rose. And as he did, on the north rim, a red pinpoint of light sparked briefly.

White Apache froze. Someone was up there. Someone smoking a cigarette. It had to be a white man keeping a watch on the canyon mouth. Conflicting emotions tore at him. White Apache tried telling himself that the man must be a lookout, nothing more. Yet if the circulars had been legitimate, there would be no need for anyone to be up there, no need at all.

The only other explanation filled White Apache with boiling rage. Whirling, he dog trotted to the north, never once exposing himself. Soon he was past the high wall. On the far side a series of slopes seemed to rear to the very sky. He prowled their base, sniffing and listening. Forty yards in, the wind brought him the scent of horses and the faint smell of woodsmoke.

White Apache climbed. His moccasins made no noise. His form was a flitting shadow, in one spot one second, in another spot the next. Many times he went to ground to test the air with his finely honed senses.

Soon White Apache came on an old game trail bearing recent horse tracks. He took it to make better time. In due course he saw a pile of dung. Squatting, White Apache picked up a piece and rubbed it between his fingers. The degree of dryness told him that the pile had been lying there for two to three days.

Above him, someone coughed.

It was faint, but White Apache instantly gauged the general area from which it came. Becoming one with the shadows, he cat footed higher. Loose earth and small stones that might slide out from under him were diligently avoided. When he halted to test the air, as he often did, he crouched and mimicked the shapes of nearby boulders or brush.

It was one of the oldest Apache tricks, the keys to their uncanny ability to sneak up on victims without being spotted.

From an early age boys were versed in the craft. They were taught how to blend into the background by assuming the guise of whatever might be around them at the time. They might, for example, kneel and curl in half, tucking their heads flush to the ground, so that their silhouette resembled that of nearby boulders. Or they might sit with their back to their prey and hold their arms and legs so that their limbs resembled those of a small tree or shrub. The possibilities were limited only by their cleverness.

White Apache had spent many hours honing his skill. He had a long way to go before he would equal the Chiricahua, but he was good enough to fool most any white-eye or Mexican.

On this particular morning, White Apache came to the crest of a rocky spine. Rolling into a ball, he inched up alongside a pair of small boulders. Below him unfolded a basin. In it were camped four white men. Only two were present, but there were four horses tethered close by, and four saddles ringed the small campfire.

One man hunkered by the fire, sipping coffee. The other was asleep, snoring lightly.

White Apache noticed that neither wore a uniform or a badge. The man by the fire, whose face was shrouded by a low hat brim, looked up. White Apache stiffened. Recognition shot through him. It was the old scout, one of the three bounty hunters he had tangled with before. He searched his memory for the name: Plunkett, that was it.

The scout glanced at the sleeper and frowned. "Belcher, you'd best get your lazy ass up and go spell Quid. I've already relieved Fergy."

The snoring choked off. The man under the blankets cracked an eye, then yawned. "Five more minutes. That's all I want."

Bob Plunkett did not hide his contempt. In his opinion, Belcher was next to worthless. Of all the men they had hired on in Tucson, the skinny gunman was the laziest. Belcher never showed up to relieve anyone on time, yet griped to high heaven if his own relief showed up so much as a minute late. Griping, sad to say, was the one thing Belcher did well. He griped about doing his fair share of the cooking; he griped about taking a turn tending the horses; he griped about practically everything under the sun.

"Don't say I didn't warn you," the scout now warned. "Quid ain't going to like havin' to wait again. He's liable to bust your skull this time."

"He doesn't scare me," Belcher said.

"Only because you don't have any brains." Plunkett went to swallow more coffee when a feeling came over him that he was being watched. He swiveled toward the canyon, thinking that Quid had returned to beat the stuffing out of Belcher. But no one was there. Mystified, he studied the north basin rim and saw nothing to account for his feeling. He looked at the horses. None showed any alarm.

Shrugging, Plunkett tilted the tin cup to his lips. Liquid splashed his neck, and he felt a slight tingling sensation. Thinking that he had stupidly missed his mouth, he wiped his throat with the back of his hand. Abruptly, the tingle changed to a searing pain, just as he raised his hand high enough to see that the warm liquid clinging to it was not coffee. It was blood. His blood.

Bob Plunkett dropped the cup and started to rise. Opening his mouth to shout a warning, he stabbed a hand at his pistol.

White Apache was faster. He clamped a hand over the white-eye's mouth, seized the scout's gun arm and held Plunkett in an iron grip. The man thrashed and fought to break free. A crimson geyser spewed from the throat White Apache had slit with a single lightning stroke. Gradually, the older man weakened. Soon Plunkett's knees buckled. White Apache eased the scout to the ground, then pinned him until the body stopped convulsing.

Bowie in hand, White Apache stepped to the skinny gunman. Crouching low, he held the bloody blade over Belcher's face. A red drop slid

161

off the cold steel, dripping onto the end of the man's nose.

The gunman snorted but did not open his eyes.

White Apache let another drop fall.

This time Belcher swiped a hand at the air, as if to ward off an annoying insect. He snorted and tossed.

Moving the blade over the man's right eye, White Apache angled it so that the next drop fell onto the eyelid.

"What the hell?" Belcher blurted, sitting up.

White Apache pounced. Slamming into the gunman's chest, he knocked Belcher flat again even as he drove the Bowie between two ribs. Belcher arched and went to scream. Instantly White Apache stifled the outcry, then savagely speared the Bowie into the gunman four more times as hard as he could. Belcher died wearing a look of dumb astonishment.

Like a tawny panther rising from its prey, White Apache stood and turned toward the canyon. Raw rage coursed through his veins. Two more men were out there somewhere. Two bounty hunters, scum who had somehow learned about his cousin and made up those fake circulars to lure him into a trap.

They were going to pay.

Chapter Twelve

Amelia Taggart was up before the sun. Taking her handbag and a towel, she slipped from her tent. The camp was quiet. None of the men were up and about yet except Wilson, whose turn it was to keep guard. He sat by the fire, his back to her, his chin bowed, dozing.

Amelia smiled. It was just as she had planned. She needed some time to herself, and there would be no better opportunity. Hastening to the spring, she went around to the far side where the shadows were deepest.

Here, Amelia hesitated. She craved a quick bath. Not since Tucson had she washed herself thoroughly, and she was tired of feeling grungy and sweaty all the time. A short dip was all she needed to be fresh and clean, at least until the sun came up and the temperature soared once again.

Amelia glanced at the gap in the boulders through which she had come. No one had followed her. But she could not help worrying about Stirco. The man had avoided her after she confronted him, but several times she had caught him giving her those same hungry looks. Given the chance, she was sure he would try something. It was up to her to deny him the chance.

After listening for footsteps, Amelia set the items she carried on a flat rock and swiftly stripped off her dress. Again she hesitated, reluctant to finish undressing for fear of being discovered. But not for long. The tranquil pool was so inviting that she shed her underthings in record time and slipped over the edge. The water was wonderfully, deliciously cool. She sank lower, kneeling, submerging herself to her chin.

No sounds came from the camp. Amelia smiled, leaned her head back and shut her eyes. The peace, the quiet and the water combined to lull Amelia into feeling momentarily secure. Leaning her head back on the rim, she closed her eyes and willed herself to relax.

Minutes went by. Amelia, savoring the exquisite sensation, did not stir. She wished that she were alone so she could stay there for hours. She promised herself that when they returned to Tucson, she would have a tub of cold water brought to her room and spend half a day in it. It wouldn't matter one whit if she resembled a prune when she was done.

Then the sole of a boot scuffed the ground. Amelia straightened. Her worst fear had been realized. Framed in the gap, leering at her, was Stirco.

"Well, well. This must be my lucky day."

"Go away," Amelia commanded.

Ignoring her, Stirco took a step toward the pool. "And if I don't, lady?"

"I will yell for Mr. Randolph."

The gunman chuckled. "Is that supposed to scare me off? Hell, that jackass couldn't beat a chipmunk in a fight. He's as useless a man as I've ever come across."

Amelia raised an arm to the rim. In doing so she exposed part of her right breast, but it could not be helped. Resting her hand near the flat rock on which her handbag sat, she made one last appeal. "This is your last warning, Mr. Stirco. I am a Taggart. I will not let you do what you have in mind."

"What are you fixing to do? Splash me?" Laughing merrily, Stirco came straight toward her.

Benjamin Quid glimpsed the crown of the sun on the eastern horizon and fumed. He should have been relieved by Belcher half an hour ago. Knowing the troublemaker as well as he did, Quid doubted that the bastard had even climbed out from under the blankets yet.

Quid was tired of waiting. He decided to go teach the no-account yack a lesson, but first he had to let Fergy know. Striding from concealment, he hiked along the edge. Far below, the canyon floor was empty.

As Quid passed a large boulder, he saw Fergy's brown hat near the top of the same cleft the pudgy gunman always hid in. Ferguson appeared to be slumped over, sleeping.

"What the hell is this?" Quid growled. "Can't anyone around here do their job right?"

The gunman from Tucson did not answer, did not even move. Angered, Quid went up and gave Fergy a rough shove. "Wake up. Damn your hide—" he began.

The big man's anger evaporated at the sight of a spreading crimson stain on Ferguson's shirt and the wide, blank eyes that were fixed on him. The gunman had been stabbed, not once but many times, in an attack so swift and vicious that Quid, 25 feet away, had not heard a thing.

"It's your turn next, bounty hunter."

The words cut Benjamin Quid to the quick. They came from behind him. There was no need for Quid to ask who it was. He knew. The White Apache had gotten the better of him a second time. It was unthinkable. It was unbearable. Firming his grip on his rifle, he tensed and whirled, hoping against hope that he could still win, that he could gun down the turncoat before the renegade did the same to him.

White Apache, though, had no intention of using his rifle or pistol. He wanted to slay the bounty hunter in personal combat, man to man. He wanted to see the look in Quid's eyes at the moment of death, to feel the life drain from Quid's body. This was the man who had duped him. This was the man who had falsely gotten his hopes up, who had stirred cherished memories which had twisted his soul into an agonized knot.

Perched on top of the large boulder, White Apache clenched his Bowie, then sprang. Quid looked up and tried to sweep the rifle higher. White Apache was on him in a flash, bowling the bounty hunter over. The Winchester clattered at their feet as they crashed into the cleft on top of Ferguson.

White Apache thrust at Quid's neck, but the big man twisted to one side, a hand dropping to his boot. Quid's Bowie flashed. Their blades met, rang, then met again. White Apache did not back up to gain more room. He was not giving any ground this day. Like a Viking of old, he was in the grip of a berserk blood lust. His sole thought was to slay the bounty hunter at any cost. Stabbing high and low, he waded in.

Quid was hard-pressed to ward off the rain of blows. The cleft was wide but not wide enough for them to move freely. His sole hope lay in getting out of there. Backpedaling as far as he could, he ducked under a slice that would have nearly decapitated him. His left hand brushed the ground. As he rose, he flung dirt at Clay Taggart's face.

White Apache dodged aside, but not quite quickly enough. His right eye seared with pain, then clouded with tears as he blinked rapidly to clear it. For a few seconds he was riveted in place.

Quid saw his chance. Pivoting, he leaped for the top, scrambling up and over. He still had his Colt. Switching the Bowie to his left hand, he drew the revolver. It was time to put an end to the White Apache's life once and for all.

Only White Apache had other ideas. In a powerful bound he cleared the top. The Colt leveled toward his chest as he flicked the Bowie, once.

Benjamin Quid saw a scarlet geyser burst from his wrist. He attempted to squeeze the trigger but his finger would not do as he wanted. His right hand had gone completely numb. Parrying another thrust with his Bowie, he retreated. Unwittingly, he backed into the boulder and could go no further.

White Apache leaped. His free hand caught Quid's left wrist. The bounty hunter managed to block his next swing. Spinning, White Apache hooked a foot behind Quid's legs and shoved. His intent was to push Quid down so that he could pin him and finish him off at leisure.

The bounty hunter guessed as much. So as he fell, he hurled himself backward, out of reach. A look of surprise came over Clay Taggart's face as

167

his flailing left arm, which should have found purchase under him, cleaved empty air. His body, instead of hitting the ground, angled downward.

In a state of shock, Quid realized that Taggart's surprise had nothing to do with his agility and everything to do with the fact that in throwing himself to the rear, he had forgotten that his back was to the edge of the precipice.

The bounty hunter plummeted, headfirst. He tried to scream, but his vocal chords were paralyzed. He saw the boulders below rush up to meet him with incredible swiftness. His last thought before he struck was that he had gone after one bounty too many.

White Apache looked down from the lofty rampart at the pile of pulverized bone and pulped flesh, then sighed. It was over. All four of them were dead. Now he could go about his business and rejoin the Chiricahua.

At that juncture, from deep within the canyon, echoed a shot.

William Randolph also heard it. Seated in his tent with a small mirror on his lap, he was clipping his mustache with tiny scissors when the crack of a pistol made him jerk around. By accident, he snipped his nose, and almost shrieked in torment.

Outside, someone cursed. Feet pounded.

Randolph jumped up. His first thought was that Apache had found them. Dashing to the flap, he peered out and saw Wilson and Carver racing toward the spring. They both stopped short when Stirco stumbled into the open, a hand pressed to his right shoulder.

"She shot me!" Stirco raged. "The bitch up and shot me!"

Randolph wasn't sure if he had heard correctly. The man couldn't possibly be referring to Amelia Taggart, could he? Randolph shoved the flap and hurried toward the trio. "What was that? Who shot you, my good fellow?"

Stirco, doubled over, moist blood staining his shirt, nearly fell. His companions caught him, then steered him toward the fire. He glanced up, his flushed features contorted in spite. "Who the hell do you think, you idiot! That she cat!"

"Miss Taggart?" Randolph said in confusion. "Why on earth would she put a bullet in you?"

"She's a Taggart, isn't she?" Stirco snarled through clenched teeth. "What more of a reason does she need?"

The reporter stood by helplessly while Carver and Wilson lowered Stirco onto his back. The latter opened Stirco's shirt, revealing that the slug had not only left a hole the size of a walnut but also shattered Stirco's collarbone.

"I can't believe she would do such a thing," Randolph said.

"Are you calling me a liar?" Stirco declared.

Rather than face the gunman's wrath, Randolph hurried to the gap and strode on through. He was so startled to see Amelia seated in the pool that he halted in amazement before noticing the cocked pistol she held. "Miss Taggart!" was all he could think of to say.

Amelia held the pistol as steady as a rock, but inwardly her emotions seethed. Not with regret over having shot a man, but with elation at how easy it had been to squeeze the trigger. She had warned Stirco. She had aimed the Derringer and given him one last chance to leave. Yet all he had done was laugh and keep on coming. Well, he wasn't laughing now.

"Miss Taggart?" Randolph repeated. "What is the meaning of all this?"

"I want some privacy," Amelia said. She was not about to launch into a full explanation, not when she was sitting there with no clothes on. "Mr. Stirco was unwilling to respect that. I hope you will."

Randolph could not take his eyes off the pistol. "Most certainly, madam." Backing out, he gave a little bow. "Never let it be said that I'm not a gentleman. We can discuss this at your leisure."

Finally alone, Amelia sagged. Her arms commenced to shake so violently that she had to set the pocket pistol down for fear of dropping it in the water. Clasping her arms to her chest, she huddled in the water, shivering not from fear but from excitement. It was a heady, intoxicating feeling, and she wondered if her cousin felt the same when he raided ranches and attacked wagon trains.

For the longest while Amelia did not move. She struggled to come to grips with what she had just done, and with herself. *Thou shalt not kill*, the Good Book said. Yet look at what she had done, and she felt good about it!

Off by the campfire an argument broke out. Amelia heard Stirco mention her name and swear lustily. He went on and on about how he was going to pay her back. The reporter said something she did not quite catch. Whatever it was, Stirco cursed louder.

For the rest of her life, Amelia Taggart would never forget what happened next. There were nine tightly spaced shots, one right after the other, *bam-bam-bam-bam-bam-bam-bam-bam-bam*. Rifle shots from high up on the north wall of the canyon. After the fourth a horse whinnied stridently and continued to do so until the very last blast. Then an unnerving silence fell.

Bewildered, Amelia strained to hear more. Something wheezed noisily, but other than that, the canyon might as well have been a graveyard. Stepping from the pool, she hastily dressed, not bothering to dry herself first. "Mr. Randolph?" she called softly. "Are you all right?"

The reporter did not reply. Clutching the pistol, Amelia sidled to the opening and saw a widening puddle of blood.

The bodies of the four men ringed the fire. All had the tops of their heads blown off, and their blood was flowing into a shallow depression. Beyond them, sprawled in a row, were the horses. One still lived, but its brains seeped from the exit wound.

Dumfounded, Amelia scanned the lofty rim. Nothing moved. No one was up there. Whoever was responsible had not seen her and gone on.

In a burst of insight, Amelia Taggart realized who it must have been. Taking a few steps, she cupped a hand to her mouth and screamed at the top of her lungs, "Clay! Clay! It's me, Amelia! Don't go! Please! We need to talk!"

Her only answer was the wail of the wind.

Epilogue

Ken Weber, the freighter, was making his first trip from Tucson to Mesilla since the day he stumbled on the two bounty hunters. He had a wad of tobacco in his mouth and a silver flask in his shirt pocket, the two essentials he could never be without on a long run. A low hill rose before him and he lifted his whip to spur the team along.

Suddenly Ken froze. He gawked. He came close to pinching himself to see if he were truly awake. For shuffling toward him down the middle of the road was a woman, a bedraggled mess of a female wearing a torn dress caked thick with dust, her hair in tangles. Dry tears smeared the dirt on her face. So shocking was the apparition that he brought the wagon to a lurching halt.

Bewildered, Ken gazed out over the empty expanse of baked country the woman must have crossed to get there. "Ma'am?" he said as she plodded toward him. "You look as if you could use some help."

The woman made no reply. Eyes fixed dead ahead, her limbs moving woodenly, she came to the team and halted. One of the mules nudged her but she never so much as blinked.

"Ma'am?" Ken said. Setting the brake, he climbed down. She did not look at him when he reached her. She did not react when he gently touched her elbow. "Can you talk, ma'am? Who are you? How did you get here?"

The woman simply stood there, arms limp, her eyes dull and glassy.

A shiver ran down Ken's spine. As carefully as he could, he guided her to the wagon and boosted her onto the seat. She never let out a peep, never moved or showed she was alive in any way. Roosting beside her, he got the wagon going again, swinging it in a wide circle that brought them back to the road with the team pointed due west instead of east.

"I'm taking you to Tucson, ma'am," Ken informed her. "My boss will throw a fit, me losing time and all, but it can't be helped."

As still as a statue, the woman stared blankly into space.

Ken Weber had seen poor souls like her before, unfortunates whose brains had been fried to a crisp by the desert sun. They were never the same again. The walking dead, a pard of his had called them.

Another shiver chilled the freighter as he cracked his long whip and headed for Tucson as if all the demons of hell were nipping at his heels.